The East Side of Lauderdale

Ken Kaye

1663 Liberty Drive, Suite 200
Bloomington, Indiana 47403
(800) 839-8640
www.AuthorHouse.com

This book is a work of fiction. People, places, events, and situations are the product of the author's imagination. Any resemblance to actual persons, living or dead, or historical events, is purely coincidental.

© 2005 Ken Kaye. All Rights Reserved.

No part of this book may be reproduced, stored in a retrieval system, or transmitted by any means without the written permission of the author.

First published by AuthorHouse 08/31/05

ISBN: 1-4208-6422-X (e)
ISBN: 1-4208-6421-1 (sc)

Library of Congress Control Number: 2005905538

Printed in the United States of America
Bloomington, Indiana

This book is printed on acid-free paper.

1.

Feet hopped and music throbbed. Young professionals, housewives, and energetic grandmothers groaned and huffed, struggling to look good in spandex. The five o'clock step-aerobics class at Female Fitness Center was in full swing.

Melinda Norman bounced in rhythm up and over a small platform, following the moves of an instructor. Sweat sprouted liberally through her tight black shorts and white tank top as she reveled in the exertion. Even after forty-five minutes, she was springing easily, her shoulder-length brunette hair flying loose, a testament to her workout discipline.

When the session was over, she grabbed a towel, wiped her face and mingled with classmates. Like everyone else, she studied herself in the wall mirror. She was extremely happy with what she saw, a rather tall, slender woman who didn't look anywhere near her thirty-six years. The mother of two little boys, she had a firm, shapely figure that constantly drew male attention.

Female Fitness made its home in a single-story brick building on Federal Highway on the East Side of Fort Lauderdale. Melinda loved this gym because it was near home, and not far from her downtown office. Best of all, it allowed only women, so she didn't have to worry about some creep gawking at her rear end.

Yet it bothered her that the studio had large picture windows, allowing the outside world to look in, particularly at night. Although located in a good neighborhood dominated by doctors' offices and professional buildings, she didn't like that someone could be out there, leering.

On this evening, she had an uneasy feeling and almost asked a club employee to walk her to her car. But she shook off this paranoia, threw on her sweatshirt, and headed out the door. Punctual by nature, she was anxious to get home and have dinner with her family.

*

In a far corner of the parking lot, two men sat in a white Ford Econoline van and watched the woman walk briskly toward her car. Both were dressed casually in slacks and sports shirts.

"Going to be fun," one said.

"Let's move," the other responded.

The van eased toward the woman's white Lexus sedan. The two men scanned the area to ensure no one was in the vicinity. They saw a woman walking towards a Mexican restaurant down the street, but she was too far away to matter.

Their intended prey unlocked her Lexus with an automatic clicker as the van rolled to a stop behind her. Melinda Norman looked up. She saw a man built like a fireplug, stocky and muscular, nonchalantly step out and approach her as though he wanted to ask a question. She immediately sensed danger and fumbled in her purse for the Mace.

But the fireplug was quick. He lunged and whipped her around by the shoulders. He put an arm around her waist and a hand over her mouth. With alarming strength, he yanked her inside the van through the cargo door. Once she was in, he slammed the door shut. Her purse flew into a dark corner, its contents jingling as it landed.

The ambush was so swift she didn't have a chance to scream.

The fireplug snatched the car keys out of her involuntarily clamped hand. Then he pinned her down on her stomach and shackled her hands behind her back with metal cuffs. He locked her ankles in chains. As she repeatedly and hysterically screamed "no," the duct tape went over her mouth.

"Calm down, ma'am," he said in a surprisingly calm voice with a slight southern accent. "We're not going to hurt you."

But all she could do was look up at him with wild eyes. Although damp with perspiration, she still smelled of the sweet expensive Chanel perfume she had worn to work earlier that day. The fireplug produced a black hood. She shook her head violently and let out a muffled shriek before he slipped it on. It had an opening near the mouth, allowing just enough ventilation to her nostrils.

Opening the van's cargo door, the man got out, rattling her keys in his hand.

"See you there," he said to the driver and slid the door shut.

The fireplug jumped in her Lexus, started the engine and backed out slowly. Then he followed the van.

*

During the ride, she continually sobbed. She wanted desperately to remain calm, to keep track of time and to be aware of light sensations through the hood, anything that might help the police later. But the feeling that she was about to be raped or killed was overwhelming. The thought of her two young sons and husband waiting for her at the dinner table, wondering where she was, made her crazy with anger and panic.

The van waded through traffic for fifteen minutes before coming to a halt. The passenger door opened and she again heard the soft, easy voice of the fireplug, the man who had grabbed her.

"That's one big garage," he said.

Garage? She could hear the whine of jet engines. They were at an airport garage. She made a mental note as the van started moving again. Ten minutes later, it stopped again.

The cargo door opened. Strong hands clamped around her upper arms as the two men lifted her out and ushered her along, as she had to shuffle in her ankle chains. She didn't resist. There was no point.

She was led up a grated metal stairway and into an enclosed atmosphere. From the smell of leather

The East Side of Lauderdale

and coffee, aromas that she was familiar with from flying dozens of times each year on business, she knew she had entered an aircraft. The men placed her in a comfortable, wide seat but left her hands shackled behind her. One of them buckled a seatbelt around her waist. The cabin door was shut. The engines came to life and the plane began taxiing. Five minutes later, it took off.

She wailed from under the hood, behind the duct tape, feeling the distance grow between her and her family. She kicked her legs, the ankle chains rattling, until she was spent and went limp with despair.

After awhile, her original abductor came back to remove the hood and gently peel the tape off her mouth. Under the cabin lights she could see that the fireplug was in his mid-twenties, had black, buzz-cut hair and weightlifter arms.

She sat forward as he removed the handcuffs. He also unlocked the ankle chains. She looked around. The cabin was large, adorned with cushy white leather chairs and couches, work desks, a TV console and a stand-up bar. Clearly, it was intended for corporate use. But she guessed that, at one time, the jet had been filled with cramped airline seats.

"Bathroom's in the back if you need it," the fireplug said matter-of-factly. "There's also coffee and sandwiches in the galley."

"Please," she said, voice quaking, "tell me why you're doing this. I have money. My husband has money. We can give you whatever you want."

The stocky fireplug seemed sympathetic.

"Be assured we are not going to hurt you—if you do as we say."

Her voice dropped to a hoarse whisper.

"Please. I have two little boys... "

He shrugged and returned to the cockpit, locking the door behind him.

*

Two hours later, the jet made a steep approach over low-level mountains and a pine forest, then landed on a private strip. It taxied to a ramp that was adjacent to an old, country lodge with a dark, wood façade and an orange-barrel tile roof. Emotionally and physically exhausted, Melinda Norman peeked at her wristwatch. It was only ten o'clock. But it felt like two in the morning.

The two men emerged from the cockpit. Now she could see the other henchman was tall and lean and also had close-cropped hair, though his was blond, and he sported a goatee. Mutt and Jeff, she thought. They helped her down the plane's built-in staircase and, once on the ramp, walked on either side.

"Why are you doing this to me?" she asked, but got no answer.

Inside the lodge, they directed her through a lobby area that featured white décor, carpeting, couches and chairs. A television rested in one corner. A security console with a bank of video screens sat in another. They marched her up a stairway to a hallway with perhaps twenty rooms.

They took her into an elegant, well-lit suite, complete with a king-sized bed, a television, and a painting of an

The East Side of Lauderdale

idyllic country scene on one wall; and a vanity mirror on another.

"You'll find the dresser and closet are full of clothes, nighties, underwear, what-have-you," the fireplug said. "There's also a refrigerator over there with everything from whisky to Snickers bars. Help yourself."

The men showed her the bathroom, which was enormous, with a glass-enclosed shower, a sunken tub and a vanity laden with toiletries and makeup. Clean towels were piled on a rack near the shower stall.

Then they started to walk out.

"Have a good night," the fireplug said.

"Pleasant dreams," the goatee said.

Tears sprouted and she screamed.

"Why? Why am I here?"

The two men looked at her sympathetically and left. As soon as she heard the door lock, she ran to twist the knob. But she was imprisoned. She charged to the window, pulled back the curtains, and yelped when she saw the steel bars. She collapsed on the bed and cried bitterly for long minutes.

She eventually peeled out of her soiled workout clothes and tossed them into a corner. She realized that if this nightmare had never happened, she would have thrown those togs into her laundry hamper in her comfortable walk-in closet at home. This made her break down and cry hysterically again.

Numbly, she washed, found a nightgown in the dresser, and slipped into bed. Despite her horrendous fear, or perhaps because of it, she slept like the dead.

*

The next morning, mellow light seeped through the window curtains. She glanced outside and saw a serene landscape of pine-covered hills in all directions. Below, she could see the jet: a Boeing 737 painted white with a dark-blue stripe over its windows. There was no corporate name on its fuselage.

Much to her surprise, she found her bedroom door was now unlocked. She donned a bathrobe and slippers from the closet and quietly padded down the stairs. In the lobby she saw the front door where they had brought her in. She was about to make a run for it when she heard the voice.

"Good morning!"

It was the fireplug. He was seated behind the lobby security console, obviously waiting for her.

"The name is Ray," he said, getting up. "Please join us for breakfast."

She nodded tentatively and looked at the door. He smiled.

"It's locked, ma'am. The house is very secure. You can go anywhere you want in here, but you won't find a way out. And if, by chance, you did manage to open a door, it would set off a very loud alarm."

She nodded again and followed him into a spacious breakfast room with tall ceilings, old-world cabinets, and a polished, wooden floor. White, linen curtains framed big picture windows and allowed outside light to filter in.

The blond man with the goatee was already at the table, eating. In the morning sun she could see that he, too, was young, almost boyish. He stood politely when she entered.

The East Side of Lauderdale

"Good morning Mrs. Norman," he said warmly. "I'm Brad. Please. Sit. Eat."

She sat down, not surprised that he knew her name. They had probably gone through her purse. Ray placed a heaping plate of scrambled eggs, bacon, wheat toast, and hash browns in front of her. He poured black coffee into her cup.

"Cream?"

"No, thank you," she said quietly.

She ate hungrily, saying nothing, and not really tasting the food.

The two men let her be, talking between themselves as they ate, recounting their flight the previous night, using technical jargon involving air traffic control procedures. She was glad they weren't focusing on her.

But after she finished, she had to inquire: "Can you tell me where I am?"

"Sure, ma'am," Brad, the goatee, said. "We're about thirty miles southwest of downtown Asheville, North Carolina, not far from the South Carolina line."

"Or Georgia," Ray, the fireplug, chimed in.

"Can you tell me who owns this lodge?"

"Rather not say."

"Is he or she the reason I'm here?"

"Soon, we'll tell you everything," Brad reassured her. "For now, here's the deal: Do exactly as we tell you and you won't be hurt. We'll fly you home soon as possible. Understand?"

She nodded, feeling a sense of relief but not trusting it.

"Good," Brad said. "I want you to go back to your room. Take all the time you need. Shower and make yourself pretty. In the closet next to the dresser you'll find a business suit like one you normally wear. Put it on."

It sounded too easy. She breathed in deeply.

"Okay," she said meekly. "Can I ask why?"

"You'll see soon enough."

Unexpectedly, she broke down and sobbed, shoulders heaving. The two men waited for her to regain her composure. Then she slowly walked upstairs.

*

An hour later, she sat on the bed in a blue business suit exactly like one she had recently purchased specifically for a feature story about her in the community newspaper. This coincidence didn't escape her. It told her that whoever had brought her to this remote lodge knew a lot about her personal affairs, right down to her exact dress size. That terrified her.

The two men entered her room, both wearing white terrycloth bathrobes and slippers. One carried a heavy, professional video camera, the kind news crews haul around. The other had spotlights and a tripod. They went about setting up the equipment around the bed.

Melinda Norman's heart kicked into high gear. She didn't like the looks of this. Why were they in robes? Why all this equipment?

"What is all that... ?"

"No questions," Brad said in a stern tone that betrayed his earlier hospitality.

The East Side of Lauderdale

The camera was positioned to capture the entire bed. Ray turned it on and a red light glared over the big lens. He focused on her sitting there with dread written on her face. He looked up and smiled soothingly, and she melted a bit, managing to smile back. Then Brad turned on the lights.

The two men dropped their robes, revealing they were naked, and the first scene would feature her screaming, trying to fend them off.

2.

To hell with it, Jeff Bruce thought.

He was supposed to meet a cop who used a helicopter, rather than a squad car, for his nightly patrol. But the guy already was forty-five minutes late and probably wasn't going to show up here at the Fort Lauderdale Executive Airport. At this time of night, the airfield, which handled only private jets and small aircraft, was quiet, with darkened hangars, deserted runways, and taxiways outlined in white and blue lights.

Bruce had been milling around the parking lot of the Fort Lauderdale Police Aviation hangar, kicking loose stones and studying the clear, October sky. He was seriously considering heading to the beach, finding a stool at his favorite bar, swirling a scotch, and listening to the ocean crash to shore. He could catch the flying cop some other time.

But then he hesitated. His stuffy young editor wanted a nice little feature on how the police were now protecting the city's most exclusive neighborhoods

The East Side of Lauderdale

with this new aerial security service. If he blew off her assignment, she'd blow her well-coifed, blonde top.

Sighing, Bruce knew it would be best to hang tight, even if it was another non-story. Since being hired by the *East Lauderdale Tattler* three months earlier, he had written about the dedication of a new tennis court, the grand opening of a jewelry store, and where the Fort Lauderdale lifeguards went for lunch. Journalistically speaking, it was all a bunch of goo.

But such was the price of being a screw-up. Not long ago he had been a respected veteran reporter at a major daily newspaper in Dallas, covering airline crashes and nuclear waste violations. Then he had been caught committing an unforgivable blunder and summarily fired. In the aftermath, no large metropolitan newspaper would have a thing to do with him. The *East Lauderdale Tattler* was one of only three small community papers that offered him a second chance, with the others being in Williston, North Dakota; and Juneau, Alaska.

As he leaned against his dark blue Volkswagen New Beetle, a cool breeze ruffled his salt-and-pepper hair. At times like this, he wondered if he should give up newspaper work rather than suffer the subtle humiliations of small-time journalism. But, at the base of him, he enjoyed reporting and writing, and, furthermore, these were the only real skills he possessed.

Clad in khaki trousers, an open-collar, white dress shirt and an old pair of Nike running shoes, he impatiently looked at his wristwatch. It was nine-thirty. Where the hell was this numbskull pilot, anyway?

He was still kicking stones five minutes later when a shiny, red Jeep Wrangler rumbled into the parking lot, skidding to a halt next to his car. Behind the wheel was a woman with thick, glossy, black hair that washed over her shoulders. Wearing a drab-green pilot jumpsuit, she hopped out and walked over.

"Sorry I'm late," she said. "Got caught in a jam on the interstate."

Jeff Bruce wrinkled his nose, something a great ape might do in the wild.

"No problem," he muttered.

She extended a hand, which was considerably bigger than his.

"Kasey Martin. That's Kasey with a 'K.' Ready to go?"

*

Under the orange glow of the security lights, she looked to be in her early thirties, though a few wrinkles at the corners of her eyes hinted that she might be older. Her nose was rather small, her lips full. Her eyes were so dark they appeared black with a slight Asian cast. Her skin was milk chocolate.

Despite the jumpsuit, he could tell she was lean and athletic. In black flight boots that laced above her ankles, she must have been at least six-foot-two, a good three inches taller than he was.

"Yes. I'm ready," he said.

"Good. Wait here while I log in. Take me just a minute."

"No rush," he mumbled.

The East Side of Lauderdale

As she walked briskly to a hangar-side office, unlocking the door and flicking on a light, he idly wondered if he had detected a slight accent. Perhaps she's Hispanic, he thought. He also couldn't help but wonder if she was married. Observant as he was, he hadn't noticed if she was wearing a wedding band. He glanced up at the sky. This is an assignment, he inwardly scolded himself, not a social opportunity. Just go for the ride.

A few minutes later, she walked out and directed him toward one of three white-and-blue Police Department helicopters parked on the flight line.

"What kind of helicopter is this?"

"Bell JetRanger, the 206B-3 model." She popped open a door and pointed at the left-side seat. "Hop in and buckle up."

He did as told, ducking into the chopper's front compartment. She walked around, strapped into the right seat, and hit some switches above her head. The helicopter's turbine engine whined to life. Strobe lights flashed, and the big rotor blades swooshed.

"Put on that headset so we can talk on the intercom," she said loudly.

Bruce slid on the headset, with its big green ears cushy against his own. He positioned a small boom microphone in front of his mouth.

After putting her headset on, she asked, "Hear me okay?"

He nodded. The headset reduced all outside noise to a comfortable level, and her voice came through clear and businesslike. He heard her ask the control tower for permission to take off. She boosted the throttle, and the concrete ramp, illuminated in the chopper's landing lights, floated away. The helicopter accelerated forward with a distinct nose-down angle.

He started to ask a question, but she put up a hand. "Not now," she said.

Okay, Bruce thought, this is going to be fun.

But at least he noticed that she wasn't wearing a wedding ring.

*

Five minutes later, they were flying over expensive homes and condos on the East Side of Fort Lauderdale. Bruce admired the lit-up swimming pools, tennis courts, city parks, and quiet streets below. Not far to the west he could see traffic snarled on Federal Highway and to the east, the dark, vast Atlantic.

"We can talk now," she said. "It's just a little busy right after takeoff."

"That's okay," he said, pulling out his notebook and pen. "Can you tell me a bit more about this helicopter?"

"The JetRanger 206 is the most popular single-engine helicopter in the world, widely used by law enforcement and the military for surveillance and training. It's powered by a Rolls Royce turbine engine, cruises at one hundred thirty miles per hour and has a maximum range of more than four hundred miles."

"Interesting," he said, scribbling, wondering if she could be anymore deadpan. Then he looked down. "Aren't we kind of high? I mean, could you see if someone was breaking into a house down there?"

The East Side of Lauderdale

"I can see fine. All I have to do is turn on my spotlight. We actually call it 'Night Sun.'" To demonstrate, she briefly turned on the searchlight, which indeed illuminated a circular patch of ground a thousand feet below quite effectively.

"But, yeah," she continued, "we are up there. Don't forget, turbine engines are loud. And those folks down there don't like a lot of noise even if they want this extra layer of security."

"You mean those rich folks, right? Why patrol over this side of town when there are so many other high-crime areas that need protection much worse?"

"Because," Officer Kasey Martin explained, "those good people down there are paying a premium for this patrol, just like they pay off-duty cops to provide security on the ground."

"How much?"

"About five hundred an hour. But, even though it was, like, once a month, the communities decided they were experiencing too many break-ins. They wanted something more than ground patrols. So the Aviation Unit took the job."

"Did you volunteer for this assignment?"

She was constantly craning her head, looking in all directions. She hesitated before answering.

"Let's just say that I like flying at night."

"So, this job is above and beyond your daytime duties?"

After more hesitation, she said, "This is my only duty for now."

He could tell she didn't want to talk about why, exactly, she was doing this low-priority task. In his previous life in Dallas, he would have pressed her. But the *East Lauderdale Tattler* wanted a public relations piece, not an investigation. He made sure the rest of his questions were nice and easy.

*

After another hour of flying lazy circles, they landed, shortly after eleven. Officer Martin skillfully lowered the JetRanger into its parking spot and killed the engine. As Bruce stepped out, he could feel his blood vibrating. He accompanied her into the police hangar office, where she filled out a flight log on the front desk. Then she locked the office, turned out the light and they walked to the parking lot.

"Things were pretty quiet tonight," he observed, as they stood near his VW under the security lights. "We didn't see any break-ins."

"Boring, you mean," she said, revealing some frustration.

"Most nights like this?"

"Usually, about the worst I see is a loose dog or a kid driving drunk."

He chuckled and asked, "How long you been a cop?"

"Five years. First three on road patrol, the last two with the Aviation Unit."

"So you learned to fly while you were an officer?"

"No. I've been flying for nine years now. Before I got into police work, I flew for a radio station in Orlando, doing traffic reports. Then I flew a couple years for the Florida Marine Patrol as a civilian and got interested in law enforcement. I ended up going to the Academy. And here I am."

The East Side of Lauderdale

"You enjoy what you do, then?"

She pushed her thick hair straight back over her head, a gesture that aroused a pang of desire in him.

"I love flying, don't get me wrong. But, to tell the truth, I'd like to be more involved in the police end of things, investigations and detective work. Right now if a bad guy comes along, I alert officers on the ground and they move in."

"You get the assist but the ground guys score the points."

She laughed, revealing a traffic jam of perfect white teeth.

"Exactly! The thing is, I want to do some good and not just fly around in circles. That's why I hope to eventually upgrade into the Detective Bureau."

He nodded.

"I'd best be going," he said, holding out a hand. "Thank you, Officer Martin. It was a great ride."

But before she could return the shake they heard a voice.

"You gonna kiss him?"

Both turned to see the silhouette of a man sitting on a Harley Davidson under the security lights about fifteen yards away. He slowly dismounted and walked toward them, gravel crunching under cowboy boots.

Bruce put a hand to his brow and saw that the unexpected visitor was at least six-foot-three and well over two hundred pounds. The man wore black jeans and a black long-sleeved shirt. He had close-cropped blond hair, a clean-shaven face and the menacing smile of a professional wrestler.

"How ya doing, Kase?"

Officer Kasey Martin, as startled as Jeff Bruce, was suddenly irritated.

"What the hell are you doing here, Jed?"

Instead of answering, he walked up close, pulled her into him and kissed her hard. She was docile for a moment but then squirmed free.

"Jesus Christ, Jed!" she said, exasperated. "I'm working, dammit!"

Bruce wrinkled his nose. He surmised that Jed must be the boyfriend he was hoping Officer Kasey Martin didn't have.

The big man laughed brusquely, obviously enjoying his intrusion.

"Working, huh? I bet."

Jed turned and gave Bruce a challenging look.

"This little fuck bothering you, Kase?"

"He's a newspaper reporter, Jed, and I'm doing an interview."

"What newspaper?"

"The *East Lauderdale Tattler*. He's writing a story about the Aviation Unit. That's the God's honest truth. That's the only thing going on here."

Eyes narrowed, Jed took a step toward Bruce, who instinctively stepped back.

"So. You're going to do a story about my sweet piece of pie here?"

"That's right," Bruce answered reluctantly.

"That's real nice."

Then Jed grabbed Officer Martin and kissed her again. This time she immediately fought to get loose and, once free, shoved Jed hard. All the coolness she

The East Side of Lauderdale

had displayed as a helicopter pilot was now replaced by indignation.

"Leave me alone, Jed! Get the hell out of here!"

Jed stood there, the defiant smile ever present.

"I'll see you later at your place. In your bed."

Then he turned and pointed a finger at Bruce's face.

"As for you, henceforth and from now on, stay clear of her."

Bruce remained quiet. Jed, a bully who knew he had won, walked back to his bike, kick-started the engine, and roared out of the parking lot.

*

Jeff Bruce and Officer Martin watched the bike's red taillight disappear.

"I'm really sorry about that," she said quietly.

Bruce nodded.

"Boyfriend?"

"He's a detective. We've been dating for awhile. I've told him not to, but he follows me sometimes. He comes over at the end of my shift to make sure I'm okay when I come out at night."

Bruce turned to her.

"He's a control freak, bordering on a stalker."

She breathed in deeply. She obviously didn't like that last word.

"Whatever he is, that's none of your business," she said sharply.

Bruce recognized the symptoms of abuse: Anger and defiance. But she was right. It was none of his business. He nodded and walked to his car.

21

After starting the engine, he looked up and saw her at his window. He rolled it down.

"I want you to know," she said, "that again, I'm very sorry about all that."

"It's okay," he said, unsure how else to reply.

Then she stared at the ground, hesitating. Bruce waited.

"There's something you should know about," she said.

"What's that?"

"A few nights ago, Friday, actually, a woman was reported missing by her husband. We think she might have been abducted. But we don't know for sure."

Bruce raised an eyebrow.

"Why do you think she was abducted?"

"Two young children. A good home life. And she was a very successful businesswoman. She had no reason to disappear. I suggest you go the Police Department tomorrow and ask for the missing person report on Melinda Norman."

"Thanks," he said, scribbling in his notebook.

He was about to ask her why she had offered this information. But when he looked up, she was already walking to her Jeep.

*

Bruce obtained the Melinda Norman report early the next morning. But it provided only meager details. He decided to work up a story just the same. From his many years in Dallas, he knew how to get around anemic police blotters.

The East Side of Lauderdale

Upon returning to the *Tattler* newsroom, on the bottom floor of a five-story office building at the corner of Commercial Boulevard and Federal Highway, he was prepared to fill his arrogant young editor in on the new development. But she wasn't there, as usual, attending some sort of social function.

That was fine by Bruce. It allowed him to delve into the Melinda Norman story without question or interruption. He checked the newspaper's archives, worked the Internet and made calls to her friends and coworkers, some of whom were unaware that she was, in fact, missing. He also tried calling her husband, Jim Norman, a bank president, but couldn't reach him.

By five o'clock, he finished the story and launched into the helicopter patrol feature. He shipped both pieces to the copy desk by six.

At seven o'clock, he was on a barstool at the beach, sipping a scotch and listening to pounding waves. Mostly, he was thinking about Officer Kasey Martin.

3.

Sheryl Tucker stretched and yawned. Peering out the French doors overlooking the Atlantic Ocean, lazing in bed, she saw the first hint of light appear on the eastern horizon. She loved this cozy calm of early morning.

Then an alarm bell clanged inside her head.

As the star columnist for the *Fort Lauderdale Post*, one of the most prestigious newspapers in the Southeast, she had no idea what she was going to write about that day. Yet she was under the gun to produce a lively, entertaining and provocative piece by that night.

Her readers expected as much. Her column, embellished with a dramatic mug shot of her oval face and piercing blue eyes, appeared three days a week on the front of the Metro section. This same photo was prominently displayed on billboards and the sides of buses. Then there were the radio and television spots, all part of a concerted campaign to market Tucker as a bona-fide celebrity. Indeed, surveys showed a vast

The East Side of Lauderdale

majority of readers turned to her corner of the paper first.

All of which set her on edge on this otherwise tranquil October morning. Where the hell was she going to find something lively and entertaining, let alone provocative?

She padded into a bathroom that was the size of most master bedrooms, splashed water in her face and tried not to despair. Something juicy would come up. But then she had been saying that a lot lately.

Her last good hit had been more than a month ago. She had discovered a city parking enforcement supervisor was forcing meter maids to provide sexual favors in return for job security. By convincing a few of the women to talk to her, Tucker built a case for the predator to be criminally prosecuted and jailed. Meanwhile, the victims won tens of thousands in compensation from the city.

This was the kind of justice Sheryl Tucker loved to dole out. When she was on her game, she was a journalistic stick of dynamite, eager to blow up the careers of crooked politicians, exploit government stupidity, and stand up for neglected poor people.

Yet too many recent columns focused on overcrowded highways and backyard spats, leaving her desperate to find a blockbuster that would pull her out of her slump. Richard Bloom, her personal valet who masqueraded as an assistant city editor, meekly suggested she take some time off and regroup. But she said no. She would hit pay dirt soon enough.

She just didn't know where.

Now she grabbed a glass of orange juice from the kitchen and returned to her bedroom. She was careful not to wake her husband, who was sleeping in his own bedroom down the hall. He might have been a fabulously wealthy industrialist, but he also was a bore. The last thing she wanted was to waste time giving in to one of his cravings.

She needed to focus on her workday. She locked her bedroom door to ensure he wouldn't surprise her, then took a long, hot shower. As steam rose around her, she ran through her options. She could hang out at City Hall or the County Morgue. She could browse the Internet, hoping for a fresh development. She could even make cold calls to key sources. But all of that would be tedious and, would likely be unfruitful.

She needed a bombshell, not a city commission follow-up. And she had no idea where to find it. Although her deadline was fourteen hours away, she already could hear the clock ticking.

As she stepped out of the shower, she decided to join her old buddies for breakfast. Who knew? Maybe one of them would have an idea.

Twenty minutes later, she was dressed in designer blue jeans, a black sleeveless top and tan high heels. She slung a Louis Vuitton purse over her shoulder and quietly escaped from the palatial home before her husband stirred.

*

Darting through rush-hour traffic on Las Olas Boulevard, Sheryl Tucker aimed her flaming-red Porsche 911 towards downtown. With the windows

The East Side of Lauderdale

down, her fashionably cut, light-brown hair buffeted in the breeze. Occasionally, young, hormonal men would honk or wave as she zipped past them.

She was, after all, stunningly beautiful, graced with the elegance and poise of a runway model. In her late twenties, she possessed full lips and a fragile nose. The eyes, while piercing, were also enticing. Her skin was a lovely olive tone, inherited from an Italian mother and a Greek father.

Some said she was angelic. Some said she was exotic. But editors and sources knew that, underneath the glamorous exterior, there was a tenacious, savvy journalist. No one dared suggest Sheryl Tucker got where she was based on her looks. She worked hard and took her craft seriously. Which was why she had her game face on this Thursday morning. She was tired of floundering.

At the Las Olas Boulevard shopping district, lined with trendy shops and cafes, she pulled into a parking lot behind the Floridian restaurant. Although it was not yet seven o'clock, a small crowd waited to be seated. The place was renowned for great food and a casual atmosphere.

Tucker worked her way to a large, round table in the back, where five stately gentlemen, all dressed impeccably in dark or gray suits, were making quiet conversation and eating their breakfasts with the slow, polite precision of the British. Seeing Tucker, smiles glowed.

"Morning, guys," she said, falling into the only open chair at the table.

"Good morning, Sheryl!" chirped Sidney Simon, chairman of the Broward County Commission, a short, balding man who had a neatly trimmed gray moustache and wore a total of five gold rings. Though more than seventy years old, he still had a gleam in his eye.

"Good morning dear," added Clayton McGreggor, an enormously successful developer who owned a South Florida sports team and was still handsome at age sixty-something. On his left wrist was a ten-thousand-dollar gold Rolex. Bifocals sat on the end of his patrician's nose.

"My lord, you look good enough to eat," chimed in Kenton Cook, who owned a national chain of family restaurants. Also in his sixties, he sported a gray beard to complement his shiny, bald dome and rotund belly.

"Sheryl," said Bradley Crawford with a nod. A retired federal judge, well into his seventies, he was the principal partner of the city's most prominent law firm. A platinum-plated cane rested by his chair. He wore wire-rim glasses holding thick lenses.

And then there was Harold Forest, the county's top prosecutor. Officially called the Broward State Attorney, he was the youngest of the group, in his late fifties. He had black-dyed hair and shocking blue eyes, thanks to the artificial color in his contact lenses.

"If only I were thirty years younger," he said in his standard greeting.

"Thank you, Harry," she said, then kissed his cheek, as he was closest. Then she cried to a nearby waitress: "Sue! Coffee! Now!"

"Be there in a minute, hon."

The East Side of Lauderdale

The old men smiled again and returned to their meals and quiet banter.

Tucker considered herself lucky to be a member of this august group. She had broken into their ranks a year earlier after writing a column about how the elderly powerbrokers met most every morning to socialize. As part of her reporting, she had joined them for a few days and was immediately "inducted" because the chemistry was so good.

As she waited impatiently for her coffee, she picked up a copy of that day's *New York Times*, searching for something that might pique her interest. The table was littered with other papers as well, such as the *Wall Street Journal* and *USA Today*, because the old gents would bring their copies from home.

After the waitress delivered a cup of black coffee, Tucker ordered her usual breakfast, a fruit cup and dry toast, then rapped an open palm on the table. The men looked up and the clinking of their silverware went silent. Seeing that she had everyone's attention, Sheryl boldly admitted, "I'm in trouble."

"As in pregnant?" Sidney Simon asked with a gleam.

"You wish," she said. "No. I'm serious. I'm in big trouble."

Clayton McGreggor asked, "What's the problem, dear?"

"I don't have a damn thing for tomorrow's paper. I need a column idea. Like now. Somebody give me something."

The distinguished gentlemen looked a bit bewildered. Considering Tucker had never before made such a request, they weren't quite sure how to respond.

Crawford, the illustrious barrister, raised a quivering hand full of liver spots.

"My firm is handling a case where the proprietor of an airboat venture is suing the state because the Everglades restoration project prevents him from going into a protected area to give airboat rides."

Tucker shook her head.

"Boring," she said, quickly adding, "but thank you, Brad."

Crawford shrugged. "Tough room," he mumbled.

Tucker turned to County Commission Chairman Sidney Simon.

"What about you, chief?"

"I know for a fact that my political opponent has been accepting thousand-dollar checks when election law says five hundred's the limit."

"Also boring. Kenton?"

"One of my restaurants in Louisiana started serving fried alligator last week. We're test-marketing it the same way McDonald's test-markets a hamburger. If it works out, we're going to put it on our menus elsewhere."

"Fried alligator?"

"Tastes like chicken."

Tucker stared at him in disbelief.

"You're bullshitting me, right?"

Kenton Cook finally laughed, and his big belly jiggled.

"Yes, I'm bullshitting you."

The entire group politely chuckled.

"Too bad, because that was close," Tucker said as the waitress placed her breakfast in front of her. She began munching on a piece of toast and elbowed the State Attorney next to her.

"Harry?"

Harold Forest was smiling with the rest over the fried alligator thing. Then he licked his lips and grew somber. Tucker put a hand on his arm.

"Hey. What's up?"

Harold Forest raised an eyebrow in a "what-the-hell" gesture. He reached over to the center of the table and picked up that morning's edition of the *East Lauderdale Tattler*. He pointed at the story stripped across the top.

"Seen this?"

*

Naturally, she hadn't. Sheryl Tucker never read the lowly *East Lauderdale Tattler*. In her opinion, and that of other mainstream journalists, it was a shopper that catered to the country-club set.

Scowling, she snatched it from Forest's hands, sat back, and read the story about the disappearance of a well-known businesswoman named Melinda Norman. When she was done, she looked at Forest.

"Did you know about this before it was published in this rag?"

"It's a police matter, Sheryl. We don't even know if a crime has been committed. We don't have any suspects. Therefore, my office has not been involved."

"Harry, you're close with the cops. You must have known about this."

Forest cleared his throat and nervously straightened his red, silk tie.

"Only bits and pieces."

Tucker threw the paper back down in the middle of the big table.

"Damn," she muttered. "A high-profile businesswoman goes missing for six days and I have to read about it in a fish wrapper."

Harold Forest looked down, avoiding her wrath.

"It's possible," attorney Bradley Crawford offered, trying to break the tension, "that there's not much to the story. This, for now, looks like a missing person case, and an awful lot of them turn out to be one spouse running away from the other."

She pointed angrily at the *East Lauderdale Tattler*, a paper that had less than a tenth of the circulation of her *Fort Lauderdale Post*.

"This stinking society newsletter says she had small children and a happy marriage. So obviously she didn't just run away. There's foul play involved."

"On the other hand," Harold Forest said quietly, "according to the story, her car is missing, too. The police aren't quite sure what to make of that."

Tucker thought for a moment.

"Is Melinda Norman the wife of Jim Norman? President of South Union Bank?"

"Yes, she is," Forest said, nodding.

"You guys looking at him?"

Forest shook his head, seemingly perturbed.

"Looking at him for what, exactly? Sheryl, he's the one who reported her missing."

"You and I both know the police look at the husband first, Harry. Maybe he had a big insurance policy on her. Maybe he caught her messing around."

Forest sighed.

"Look. Again, my office isn't involved. I don't have any details."

"Who does?"

Tucker knew she was on the verge of crossing a line. She considered the men at this table to be friends, and they considered her a daughter. Now she was acting as a journalist and treating them like sources.

Harold Forest again licked his lips.

"I tell you this only because of our close relationship, Sheryl. I tell you this in hopes that you will not reveal where you heard it."

"Jesus, Harry, that goes unsaid. Just spill it."

"Yes, the police do think she was abducted. The lead detective working this case is Carlos Pena. If you'd like, I'll arrange it so you can call him directly without going through the PIO," he said, referring to the police information officer.

Tucker finished her coffee and smiled.

"I'd appreciate that."

Forest nodded, still uneasy.

But Tucker leaned over and kissed his cheek again, and this brought relief to the whole table. They could see that she was more excited than irritated, having found her column idea. It didn't matter to her that the *Tattler* had the story first. It was such a small publication that nobody read it anyhow.

As she got up to leave, Tucker picked up the *Tattler* again. She pointed at the byline under the Melinda Norman story.

"Who the hell is Jeff Bruce?"

4.

From the address listed on the police report, Bruce found the Norman home off Middle River Drive, squatting next to the Intracoastal Waterway. It was a single-story structure with a white-stucco exterior and black shutters. Like many of the properties in this exclusive neighborhood, the lawn was painstakingly manicured. A forty-foot Hatteras was docked in back.

He turned into a half-circle driveway and parked behind a silver BMW 740, possibly belonging to Jim Norman. Wearing dark sunglasses, Bruce walked up to the double front doors, guarded by two marble cherubs.

He rang the doorbell twice. It was more than a minute before one of the double doors swung open.

"What?"

Raw agitation was etched into every line of Jim Norman's face. Graying and tanned, he wore casual clothes suited for the golf course.

"Mr. Norman, I'm Jeff Bruce, a reporter for the *East Lauderdale Tattler*."

The East Side of Lauderdale

"So what?"

"I'd like to talk to you about your wife."

Jim Norman stared at him.

"No."

The door began to swing closed until Bruce slapped a palm against it.

"Hey, what are you—?"

"Mr. Norman," Bruce said evenly, "I don't appreciate people slamming doors in my face, and I don't care how much money and power they have."

Some of the anger drained from Jim Norman's eyes.

"Look, I'm having a hard time. What did you say you want?"

"To talk to you about your wife, about what she was doing before she disappeared. I don't know if you saw our story about her disappearance today, but it's obvious she's an important person, high-profile in the community."

Jim Norman studied Bruce.

"Yes, I saw the story," he said quietly.

The door opened wider.

*

Southwestern turquoise and sunset colors dominated the spacious home. The floor was Mexican tile. Leafy plants sulked in the corners and big picture windows gazed out onto a screened-in pool.

Norman led him into a den, where framed photos of Melinda and their two boys dominated one wall. He pointed to a leather chair, and Bruce sat down.

"She's been gone almost a week now," Norman said, falling onto a nearby couch, casting tired eyes down. "Last night, I took the kids to their grandmother's because I didn't want them to see me like this."

"How's that?"

Norman looked up at him.

"All fucked up."

Bruce tucked away his sunglasses and pulled out his notebook and pen.

"Tell me about her."

Norman smiled sadly.

"She put in fifty hours a week as vice president of IRL Corp., which happens to be one of the biggest electronics firms in the southeast. She did a lot of volunteer work. She worked out regularly. But she always made family priority. No way did she just up and leave. But the police say that's a possibility."

Bruce noted that he was talking about his wife in the past tense, which probably meant nothing, but could have been a subconscious slip-up—if he in fact knew Melinda Norman was dead.

"If she was abducted, who might want to do such a thing?"

Norman shook his head.

"She was successful, pretty, full of vigor. She was a target for any weirdo who … " Suddenly, he hunched over and sobbed, face in hands. He eventually pulled out a handkerchief and wiped his eyes. "Sorry."

"Jim, I know this is a bad time," Bruce said, gingerly shifting to a first-name basis. "But can you tell me when you last saw her?"

The East Side of Lauderdale

"Friday morning. We had breakfast; me, her, the boys. We made sure the boys caught their bus. Then we both left for work. I kissed her goodbye."

"That was it?"

"Not quite. She called me about eleven that morning to remind me to be home by six. She was making pot roast and didn't want me to be late. That was the last I heard from her."

"Did she sound unusual in any way?"

Norman shook his head.

"She sounded fine. She didn't sound like she was planning to run out on me, if that's what you mean."

"Just asking questions, Jim."

"Just like the cops."

"Do you know if she actually went to work that day?"

"Yes. The detectives interviewed people at her office. She ate lunch at her desk and went to her five o'clock aerobics class."

"Did she go to that class often?"

"Five times a week at Female Fitness Center."

"So she was in pretty good shape."

Norman let out a pained chuckle.

"You should have seen Mindy in her workout outfits. Incredible."

"Where is this fitness center?"

"Imperial Point Plaza over on Federal. The cops told me she attended the entire class. They think she might have been confronted in the parking lot there, because that was the last time anyone saw her."

"What do you think happened to her car?"

"I think whoever abducted her forced her to drive someplace. Probably at gunpoint because she wouldn't have gone easy."

That thought brought a long moment of silence.

"Jim, is there any chance she was kidnapped? For ransom?"

"Unlikely. The cops said I would have heard from the kidnappers three days ago. So where the hell does that leave her?"

Bruce shrugged sympathetically.

"I'm sorry," was about all he could manage to say.

Jim Norman starred idly at the Mexican-tile floor.

"Me, too."

*

As he drove back to the *Tattler*, Bruce thought about Jim Norman, a bank president reputed to be a tough businessman. He seemed sincere enough, but something wasn't quite on the level. Maybe it was the sob; it seemed staged.

Bruce guessed that the police had an eye on Jim Norman. They always looked at the spouse first. Yet it was hard to believe Norman possessed a motive to kill such an attractive, dynamic wife who was the mother of his children.

The *Tattler* newsroom was quiet that Thursday morning. A few reporters sat at their computers, settling into their workday. He rarely talked to any of them. He knew they thought of him as an outsider, an older person who didn't quite belong. Otherwise, the place reminded Bruce of an insurance office: sterile, compact and full of little cubicles.

The East Side of Lauderdale

Seated at his desk, he glanced at the morning edition and saw that the flying patrol story had been played on the front page, accompanied by a large photo of Officer Kasey Martin standing by her chopper in broad daylight. The photo had been shot by the Police Department and sent to the *Tattler*, which made Bruce grin. The paper had been too cheap to send its own photographer on the night he rode with her.

Above the aerial patrol piece was his exclusive story on Melinda Norman.

Not a bad day's work, he thought.

He noticed his phonemail message light was blinking and tried to ignore it. He was eager to start writing a follow-up on Melinda Norman's last movements and include her husband's conviction that she had been abducted.

But the light kept blinking. Fearing that it might be a detective returning his call, Bruce retrieved the message. He stiffened when he heard her voice.

"Hello, Mr. Bruce. This is Officer Martin. First, thank you very, very much for the great story today. The whole Aviation Unit appreciated it. I have some information that I think you'll find interesting. But I don't feel comfortable giving it over the phone. Could meet me, say at four o'clock, at the basketball courts on the beach at Las Olas? I think you'll find it worth your while. Thanks."

Baffled, he stared at his phone. Though curious about what information she might have, he was more intrigued that she had thought to call him at all, even if he had placed her on the front page of the *Tattler* that day.

*

After gobbling down a meatball sub for lunch, Bruce spent the better part of the afternoon pounding on his keyboard. At three o'clock, he electronically shipped his Melinda Norman story to a computerized basket. From there, his young, persnickety editor normally would have perused it. But once again, she wasn't in the newsroom that afternoon, likely attending some soiree. Bruce made sure the copy desk knew the story had been turned in and bolted out.

He arrived at the beach twenty minutes early, parked in a city lot, and walked toward the basketball court, an island of asphalt surrounded by sand. The players, mostly shirtless, were bounding up and down the court with hoots and howls with each shot made or missed. It was high-energy competition, which made Bruce somewhat envious. The only exercise he really enjoyed was walking, and he didn't do that enough.

He glanced around for her tall frame clad in a pilot jumpsuit. But she was nowhere in sight. He meandered to the court's edge and sat on a bench to watch the game. It wasn't until he looked closer that he noticed a tall, black woman in the middle of the fray, battling for rebounds and making long jump shots.

Suddenly, Bruce realized the woman was Officer Kasey Martin. Her hair was pulled back severely into a ponytail, which switched back and forth as she bounded with the ease of a gazelle. She wore black gym shorts and a red tank top, revealing a hard, flat tummy. Her skin was glistening with sweat.

When she saw him, she put a hand up to the other players, indicating she was taking a timeout. She

The East Side of Lauderdale

walked over, grabbed a hand towel from a duffel bag next to Bruce's bench, and wiped her face.

"Hi there," she said, not breathing hard at all.

"Hello," Bruce said, standing up, again noting that she dwarfed him.

"Thanks for coming. Let's walk a bit if you don't mind."

"Sure."

They strolled toward the surf, a southeast breeze making the air feel cool. Seagulls were crying and splashing in the surf.

She asked, "We off the record?"

"If that's how you want it."

"They found her car. A white Lexus."

"Melinda Norman's car? Where?"

"Fort Lauderdale-Hollywood International. Fifth floor of the garage."

"Who found it?"

"A Broward Sheriff's deputy on airport detail spotted the plate last night."

"Any evidence of foul play?"

"Nothing. But the crime scene people did find something interesting."

"What?"

They had come close to the water and Officer Martin stopped to look at him with intense dark eyes. Was that Filipino he saw in them?

"I need to be sure. You didn't hear this from me, right?"

"Absolutely."

"The ticket stub. You know—the one that comes out of the ticket spitter. For whatever reason, it was left on the seat. That's what they found."

Bruce was confused.

"That's interesting but what does—"

Then he knew.

She continued, "The card was punched in at 7:26 p.m. on October fifteenth. That at least gives us a time frame."

"So it does." He pulled out his notebook from a back pocket. "I'm not going to quote you. I just want to remember that time and date."

She nodded.

He asked, "So, what's the theory?"

"Unfortunately, nothing is clear-cut. While we still think she was abducted, it's possible she caught a flight. On the other hand, we checked with the airlines and her name doesn't appear on any passenger manifests, at least on that day."

"She might have used another name."

"Yes. Or she might not have gone on a flight at all. She might have parked the car and taken a cab. Or was picked up by someone. But if she was abducted, the perps might have parked the car there, knowing it would be awhile before it was found. It's a damn big garage."

After jotting this down, Jeff Bruce looked up. He noticed how wisps of hair fell over her forehead fluttered in the breeze.

"Why are you telling me this?"

She shrugged.

The East Side of Lauderdale

"If Melinda Norman's story is put out there, somebody with information might come forward. Unfortunately, my superiors probably wouldn't agree. So that's why I need to talk to you in a somewhat secretive manner."

"I see. But why the *Tattler*, then? The *Post* has many more readers."

"I don't trust the *Post* to keep my name out of it. And you did such a nice job with the story about our helicopter patrol that I thought of you first. I must say you made me look pretty good."

He held back an impulse to tell her he didn't need to make her look good, that she was already magnificent.

Instead, he said, "It sounds like you're directly involved with the case. I thought you told me all you did was fly for now."

"Let's just say I'm close to the situation."

He wanted to explore what she meant by that. But he decided not to push it. He stuck out his hand.

"I'm grateful that you thought of me."

She returned the shake with the same crunching grip, albeit a touch sweatier.

"You're most welcome. Goodbye, Jim."

"Bye," he muttered, watching her run back to the basketball court, only a little disheartened that she didn't remember his name.

He walked slowly back to his Volkswagen, knowing he had to return to the *Tattler* and make an addendum to his story.

Melinda Norman's car had been found at the airport.

5.

The *Fort Lauderdale Post* was a major corporation with more than ten news bureaus in Florida, as well as outposts in New York, Washington, D.C., and San Juan. Its downtown headquarters filled five full floors of a massive high-rise, and the newsroom, on the eleventh floor, took the lowest of these.

Shortly before nine o'clock that Thursday morning, Sheryl Tucker stepped off the elevator and into the newsroom foyer. As usual, she arrived well before most other editorial workers, greeted only by the hum of computers. She walked briskly past row after row of empty cubicles and assorted work areas until reaching her corner office. Unlocking the door, she flopped down in a cushy, brown-leather, executive chair behind a modern mahogany desk.

Then she tilted back her head and yelled.

"Richard! Get in here!"

Richard Bloom sighed. He closed out the solitaire game on his computer screen and moseyed over to her office, which was next door to his. Despite their

The East Side of Lauderdale

proximity, her office had a beautiful view of the ocean and distant condos, while his overlooked rooftop cooling vents.

He leaned against her doorway, holding a mug of coffee.

"'Morning, your highness."

"Up yours, Richard. You seen this?"

She held up the copy of the *East Lauderdale Tattler* that she had stolen from the breakfast table and pointed at Jeff Bruce's story on Melinda Norman's disappearance.

Bloom took the paper from her and sank into a couch across from her desk. He read and casually sipped his coffee. His tie was loose and his white shirt was unbuttoned at the collar. He had plenty of time before the big bosses arrived to pull the tie tight and reapply some gel to his buzz-cut brown hair.

Meanwhile, a newsroom clerk, a young man with a ponytail, delivered, without prompting, a cup of black coffee to Tucker's desk. She didn't even acknowledge his existence as he quietly entered and departed.

When he finished reading, Richard Bloom looked up.

"So they got a story about a *possible* abduction," he conceded. "Looks like a nice little story for the police reporters."

"That," Tucker said forcefully, "is exactly what I was afraid you'd say. Richard, look, this has potential. She's a powerful businesswoman, a big name in society circles and it appears she's been abducted. Maybe murdered. I think that warrants more than a brief."

In the past month, Bloom had heard Tucker promoting a lot of offbeat developments. In most cases, they were dead ends and he had to talk her into going in another direction. He reread the top of the Melinda Norman story.

"Yes, but for now she's just missing. There's no firm evidence of foul play. She might have run off with a lover. She might have escaped from a lousy home life. What you may think is a sensational homicide could be nothing more than a marital spat. We can't exactly react to what this rag has to say," he said, tossing the *Tattler* back on her desk.

Sheryl Tucker's eyes burned through him.

"Listen, Richard. This is what I want you to do. I want you to go into the eleven o'clock meeting and tell those brain-dead editors I'm handling this. Then tell the cop reporters to keep their grubby little paws off of it."

Richard Bloom gripped his coffee cup with both hands.

"Okay," he said after some hesitation, "but even if she was abducted, I certainly hope you don't attempt to implicate someone before the police do so."

"The husband is always a good bet. Maybe he caught her screwing around on him and put a contract out on her. And that reminds me; the husband is none other than Jim Norman, president of South Union Bank. A very rich, powerful, behind-the-scenes kind of guy."

"Which means he has plenty of money to file a defamation of character suit. I don't understand. What makes this worthy of commentary rather than a police

The East Side of Lauderdale

story? What kind of slant could you possibly put on this?"

She furrowed her brow.

"I don't know yet," she muttered. "But by deadline I will."

*

Detective Carlos Pena was expecting Tucker. His commanding officer had called and instructed that she be extended every courtesy, which, in turn, had been at the request of State Attorney Harold Forest.

The detective politely stood as she walked breezily into his second-floor hutch in the Fort Lauderdale Police Station. In his mid-thirties, with thick, jet-black hair and a face that was all angles, Pena shook her hand and asked her to have a seat. She sat in a hard-back chair across from his desk, noting his office had the claustrophobic feel of a broom closet.

"What can I do for you, Miss Tucker?"

"It's Mrs. Tucker, but you can call me Sheryl. You can start by telling me what really happened to Melinda Norman."

"What *really* happened? I'm not sure I understand, Sheryl."

"I'm wondering if the husband had a motive for offing her. Was she having an affair? Was she threatening to divorce him and take half his estate?"

Pena chuckled.

"You've made quite a leap. No one said the husband offed her. Truth is we're not even looking at Jim Norman. As far as we know, he had no motive and she wasn't messing around on him."

Detecting a mild Cuban accent, Tucker found herself somewhat charmed by Carlos Pena. The guy was, if nothing else, straightforward.

"Carlos, listen. We both know Melinda Norman was abducted and probably murdered. I'm just asking you to tell me what you got."

Pena put both elbows on his desk and clasped his hands together.

"For the record, all we know is that Melinda Norman is a hard-working businesswoman, a good mother and a loving wife. She is not the kind of woman who would suddenly leave everything behind. But we don't have any hard evidence that she was abducted."

"How about off the record?"

"Off the record, we have a witness."

Tucker raised an eyebrow.

"Really," she said, fishing her notebook out of her purse. "Go on."

"She's a waitress who works at a Mexican restaurant near the fitness center where Mrs. Norman took her aerobics class. The wit was just arriving to start her evening shift when she thought she saw a man pull a woman into a white van."

"And you think that woman was Melinda Norman."

"Yes. The waitress provided a pretty solid description of her."

"Any description of the man who grabbed her?"

"Short hair, clean shaven, dressed casually, or so the wit said."

"Can you give me the name of this witness?"

"Rosa Perez. Nice woman, actually."

The East Side of Lauderdale

Tucker gently tapped the end of her pen on her notebook.

"This all sounds fairly cut-and-dried, Carlos. You have a witness who clearly saw a woman forced into a van. Why are you so hesitant to go on the record and say it's an abduction?"

"Because of one little thing: Mrs. Norman's car was found at the airport last night. So it is entirely possible that our witness saw some other woman pulled into the van while Mrs. Norman drove to the airport and caught a flight."

Tucker threw her hands up, exasperated.

"Come on, Carlos. Stop bullshitting me."

Carlos Pena didn't blink. Giving her too much inside information would endanger the investigation.

"Look, here's where we're at: The car, a white Lexus, has been towed to our compound for inventory and forensic evidence. They found the ticket-spitter stub in the car, but it doesn't give us much to go on. If the techs find something else, maybe we can confirm abduction. Until then, we just don't know."

She wrote this down and looked up at him.

"Why in the hell wasn't something released to the media three or four days ago? She's been missing almost a week and there's a ton of people who might have offered information if they knew about her disappearance."

Detective Carlos Pena shrugged.

"We didn't feel we had a situation that warranted media attention."

Tucker stood up, put her palms his desk and leaned toward him.

"Then here's the big question: Why did this story first appear in the *East Lauderdale Tattler*? Why did someone from this department leak sensitive information to such a diddly-squat newspaper?"

Unfazed by her close approach, Carlos Pena shook his head.

"I have no idea."

She looked at him accusingly.

"Right."

Then she walked out.

*

Tucker tracked down Rosa Perez, the waitress who was working the early shift that day at a restaurant called Over the Border. Perez, a rather heavyset woman and a native of Venezuela, was more than willing to recount what she had already told the police.

After a quick lunch, Tucker then talked to Melinda Norman's workout partners at the Female Fitness Center. In the early afternoon, she went to the victim's place of business, IRL Corp., in downtown Fort Lauderdale and interviewed her bosses and co-workers.

Finally, Tucker focused on Jim Norman. She dropped by his bank office but was told he wasn't working that week. When she went to the Norman home, no one answered the door, even though there was a silver BMW in the driveway. Later, back at her office, she was unable to reach him by phone, which made her all the more suspicious that the husband was involved.

The East Side of Lauderdale

At five o'clock, she locked her office door to minimize disruption and began writing. At seven o'clock, she had dinner delivered to her desk: a cheeseburger, salad, and an iced tea from a downtown restaurant, working as she ate. At nine o'clock, she poked her head in Richard Bloom's office. He had been patiently playing solitaire, his tie and shirt collar again loosened.

"It's yours," she said.

She returned to her office and waited for him to edit her column. She retrieved a bottle of Chardonnay from a small refrigerator under her desk and poured the wine into a plastic cup. Alcohol was strictly forbidden anywhere on the premises of the *Fort Lauderdale Post*. Except in Sheryl Tucker's office. She turned on a wall-mounted television, collapsed on her couch, and watched the evening edition of CNN.

Bloom, meanwhile, punched up her piece on his computer screen. Normally, her copy was tight, well-organized, and started with a roundhouse punch to the reader's jaw. This one was no different:

For all anyone knows, Melinda Norman is chained to a bed somewhere, naked, beaten, bleeding, and dying. Or, worse, she could already be dead.

Or, she could be on the French Riviera, sipping champagne and whispering sweet nothings to a lover.

The problem is, we just don't know.

However, the former is considerably more likely because a witness apparently saw her being tossed into a van in a dark parking lot last Friday night.

And the police, as well as her husband, bank tycoon Jim Norman, president of South Union, kept their mouths shut for all this time. Maybe they didn't want to look foolish if Melinda showed up. Or, maybe they know some details they would rather not reveal.

One way or the other, someone is going to look bad—extremely bad—if her body turns up.

If Jim Norman—who seems to have gone into hiding, by the way—and the police had thought to put the story out there sooner, without the hush job, someone might have provided critical information leading to her whereabouts.

Melinda Norman is the mother of two small boys. She is the vice president of IRL Corp., one of the region's leading electronics distributors. And she is a popular community activist who has helped raise thousands in charity for various organizations.

In fact, she is so well known that it's amazing that any number of people, including coworkers, friends, and workout partners, didn't come forward to ask:

Just where in the hell is Melinda Norman, anyway?

Now I ask, just how long were the cops and the hubby going to sit on this?

It went on to talk about the witness and how the car was found at the airport, as well as to provide more background on Melinda Norman. Shortly before ten o'clock, Bloom shipped the column to the copy desk, where it went into the maw of a giant production machine with editors scrutinizing it, placing a headline over it, and sizing it for the next day's paper.

The East Side of Lauderdale

His job done, Bloom leaned on her door, hands in pockets.

"Hell of a good piece," he said quietly. "I think it's safe to say you've come out of your slump."

Tucker was sipping on a second glass of wine.

"Is it going out front?"

She was referring to the front page: "One-A."

"It certainly is."

She nodded, gulped down the rest of her spirits, and got up.

"Great. Goodnight, Richard."

"Goodnight, your highness."

Richard Bloom watched her walk to the elevators, then he returned to his office to play one last game of solitaire. Many in the newsroom thought he was gay because he was so prim. But at that moment he was intensely jealous of the man who would spend the night with Sheryl Tucker.

*

When Tucker got home, well past midnight, her husband, Bob, was in his den, doing some paperwork. He was clad in pajamas and a smoker's jacket, because once in awhile he actually would smoke a pipe. This was his favorite room, and it was common for him to labor at his desk for hours on end.

He brightened when he saw her walk in.

"Good evening, my dear," he said. "You're looking as lovely as ever."

Which in the parlance of their marriage meant that he was in the mood.

You little creep, she thought. He reminded her of a hamster with beady little eyes. He also had a mealy-mouth way about him that disturbed her. At one time she thought she actually loved him. But that was when she was much younger, taken with an older man's wealth and power. Now the thought of intimacy with him made her nauseous.

"Not tonight," she muttered and turned away.

Bob Tucker said nothing as he watched her walk slowly toward her room. He heard her door close and the lock click into place.

6.

Bright sun and a stiff breeze greeted Jeff Bruce as he grabbed the *Fort Lauderdale Post* off the catwalk in front of his apartment on Friday morning. Squinting, he retreated back into his kitchen where it was pleasantly dim, thanks to venetian blinds. Still in his bathrobe, Bruce opened the paper on a countertop, studied the huge headline, and wrinkled his nose.

WITNESS SEES WOMAN ABDUCTED

He read halfway through Sheryl Tucker's column before the paper went straight up, smacked the ceiling and rained down onto the well-worn linoleum floor. He fell into a chair at his small coffee table, slapped his hands to his face and rocked back and forth. Tucker had murdered him.

She had liberally quoted witness Rosa Perez, who all but confirmed that Melinda Norman had been abducted. She had police sources saying they were trying to identify fingerprints in the victim's car. She had detailed background on Melinda Norman's career and social work. And she slammed Jim Norman and the cops for waiting almost a week to reveal Melinda Norman was missing.

Collecting himself, he read her column carefully from start to finish. At least she didn't have any quotes from Jim Norman, while he had managed to conduct a full interview. But so what, he thought. Nothing the tiny *Tattler* published could upstage the huge and ponderous *Fort Lauderdale Post*.

Bruce got up and surveyed his forlorn little apartment, its barren walls and cheap furniture. It told of an empty man filled with frustration. He was forty-two now, an age when most people were settled into life. Yet he was struggling in so many ways.

He meandered to the window and opened the blinds just enough to see the wind rustling the palms in the courtyard in front of his apartment building. He could hear the whoosh of traffic on Interstate 95, only a block away. Lonely sounds. He thought about his father, the eternal optimist, who firmly believed that if you try hard enough and work long enough, you can accomplish anything you want. His father had been a prominent heart surgeon and enjoyed all the richness of life: a beautiful wife, good friends, expensive cars, membership in an exclusive country club, and a posh home in an upscale Detroit suburb. But so far, trying hard hadn't been enough for Jeff Bruce, and at times like this he was grateful that the old man had died before seeing his only son flounder.

Bruce turned away from the window and slumped back into the chair. He picked up the mangled *Post*

The East Side of Lauderdale

from the floor and admired Tucker's intense glare in the photo that accompanied her column. His snotty young editor probably wouldn't even notice that he had been beaten so badly because she wasn't interested in serious news. Yet his pride told him that he should have gotten to that witness first and he should have gotten better information.

He fidgeted in misery for several more minutes before realizing something. Tucker had failed to report an important detail: the ticket-spitter stub found on the front seat of Melinda Norman's Lexus. He had opted not to include that in his story, sensing it might be important later, and perhaps even give him an edge.

*

He arrived at the *Tattler* at nine o'clock and saw that his editor was already in her office. Hoping she wouldn't see him, he slipped into the back room where copies of that day's *Tattler* were stacked for staff use. He took one back to his cubicle, anxious to see how his Melinda Norman story was played. If it was on the front page, he wouldn't feel quite so belittled by Tucker.

But it wasn't there. He had to flip through several pages before he finally found it—severely cut. He shut his eyes, stinging again.

"She killed you."

Bruce looked up to see his editor, Samantha Pauline VanDermark, or Sam, as she was called around the newsroom, standing over him.

"What do mean?" he asked, knowing full well what she meant.

"Sheryl Tucker. She killed you today."

"Yes, I know, Sam. I saw the Post," he responded, surprised that she was berating him, the woman who didn't even know how to spell hard news.

"She made it her story even though you broke the whole thing yesterday."

"I'm aware of that, Sam."

Sam, who had fashionably shagged, startling blond hair, wore a glowing pink skirt and matching jacket, one of her many vogue outfits. She was a lot of flash and not much substance, Bruce thought. He often wondered how, at the tender age of twenty-six she had landed the job of editor, even at a small shop like the *Tattler*. She lacked the skills and seasoning, and that was reflected almost daily in bad news decisions and misplaced priorities. But she had gone out on a limb and hired him, so he felt somewhat beholden to her.

Now she huffed at his insouciance.

"I'm very disappointed, Jeff. We look silly today. We look like we're trying to compete with the *Post*. But they do crime and murder and we do tea parties and grand openings. You knew that when I hired you. That's why I'd like you to back away from this Melinda Norman thing and do what I hired you to do: write nice stories about nice people in our community. And try shaving once in awhile."

"What?" He rubbed his chin, feeling two days of stubble.

"Look, Jeff, truth is I can't afford to have you chasing after this abducted woman. As far as I'm concerned, that's not a good use of your time. You gave it your best shot and you fell short."

The East Side of Lauderdale

Despite his dumbfounded look, she continued, "I need you to interview Betty Sue Curtis this morning. As you may or may not know, she's the host of a home shopping show on WBLS, the local cable station. I would like you to work up a profile on her for the Monday paper."

He stared at her in disbelief but knew she was right. He knew what the job entailed when he was hired.

"Okay," he said quietly. "I'll do a profile on this cable woman. But, please. Let me stay on the Melinda Norman story, Sam. It's important to me. And I think it will be good for our newspaper."

Samantha Pauline VanDermark impatiently tapped one of her pink, high-heel shoes, purchased for three hundred dollars at Bloomingdale's.

"Okay. But let's get something straight: If this abduction thing gets in the way of anything I assign, well, let's just say I'm not going to be happy. You understand what I'm saying, Jeff?"

"Yes, Sam. I do."

*

From years of pressure-cooker experience, Bruce was able to drive to the cable station, interview Betty Sue Curtis and pull together a profile in less than three hours. In the process, he skipped lunch, but he wasn't all that hungry.

Now he could refocus on Melinda Norman—and that ticket stub. Seeking a first-hand look at the scene, he drove to Fort Lauderdale-Hollywood International Airport in mid-afternoon and wound his way to the fifth level of the garage. There he found the empty spot where her Lexus had been parked, cordoned off with yellow crime-scene tape.

He parked nearby, got out, and studied the area. Happily, the garage was quiet, with few cars coming or going. Out on the runway, jets roared into a cloudless blue sky, aiming toward the Atlantic. The first question that came to mind: Why had the abductors left her car here? Bruce figured it was because they had taken a flight out and weren't concerned that the car eventually would be found. If so, the next question was whether Melinda Norman had been forced to go with them or had been killed, her body discarded along the way.

Bruce pulled out his notebook and found where Officer Kasey Martin had said the ticket had been pulled from the spitter at 7:26 p.m., that Friday, exactly a week ago now. Meanwhile, according to Tucker's column, the witness supposedly saw the Norman woman yanked into a van at about 6:30 p.m., in northeast Fort Lauderdale. In other words, it had been less than an hour from the time Melinda was last seen alive to the time her car arrived at the airport.

That didn't leave the abductors much time to kill her and ditch the body. Which would suggest she had been forced onto a plane alive. But it must have been a private plane, Bruce reasoned, because it would have been impossible to get her on an airliner at gunpoint or knifepoint in light of tight security.

The only logical conclusion, then, was that she and her abductors had boarded a private plane, probably at a private hangar, where security was lax or nonexistent. He further surmised that this plane took off at least thirty minutes after the Lexus entered the garage. It

The East Side of Lauderdale

would take that much time to drive from the garage to a hangar and then discreetly get her on board an aircraft.

If his assumptions were right, the getaway plane probably didn't lift off until eight p.m., and probably no later than nine p.m. That gave him some loose parameters to work with.

He hopped back in this VW, anxious to take the next step.

*

He drove to the west side of the field and parked at a five-story building called the Fort Lauderdale Jet Center. It was home to companies that provided fuel, maintenance, and catering services, primarily to corporate jets. It also housed the Flight Standards District Office, an agency that monitored the skies, coming under the Federal Aviation Administration.

He asked a clerk at the front counter for the office manager and waited fifteen minutes before a balding man with turtle-rim glasses appeared.

"Charlie Benson. What can I do for you, sir?" No hand was extended.

"Jeff Bruce from the *Tattler*. I'd like to see the log of flights that departed here last Friday. I'm trying to determine if a certain private plane flew out that night for a story I'm working on," he said, not revealing the whole truth.

"You talk to our media relations staff, Mr. Bruce?"

"No, sir. I was hoping to circumvent some bureaucracy."

Benson hesitated. Then he said, "Going to take some time for that."

"I can wait."

A half an hour later, Benson reappeared with a computer printout. As Bruce came over to look at it, he noticed that Benson smelled of cigar smoke.

"This," the FAA man said, "is not allowed to leave the office. But you can sit here and look it over. Just don't mention where you saw it."

"Thanks, Mr. Benson," Bruce said, grateful that there were still some no-nonsense people left in the world.

Benson returned to his office while Bruce sat in the foyer and studied the "Tower Ops" log. Each line listed a flight, which was categorized as either airline, military or general aviation. Then came a tail number and a takeoff or landing time. Finally, the log provided the destination for departing flights and the originating city for those arriving.

On the night in question, seventeen planes departed between eight and nine p.m. and another fourteen in the following hour. Bruce painstakingly wrote down the information on each. But he would concentrate on the private flights in that eight o'clock hour, and there were only seven of those.

He left the computerized log with the front counter clerk and yelled "thank you" toward Charlie Benson's office. But there was no response.

*

Upon returning to the *Tattler*, Bruce grabbed a Diet Coke out of a vending machine and set out to find the registered owners of those seven private flights based on their tail numbers. It took him less than an hour to

The East Side of Lauderdale

do so, using an Internet database search. In the process, he discovered that only three of them were corporate jets, while the others were smaller prop planes.

He decided to zero in on the jets, working on a hunch the abductors had significant resources. One was a Gulfstream IV headed to Las Vegas, operated by a Delaware firm. Another was a Learjet that zipped to Chicago, owned by a large retail company. The last was a Boeing 737, owned by a concern called RTE Inc. of Fort Lauderdale. It had flown to Asheville, North Carolina.

A Boeing 737 used as a private plane? Bruce found that curious. For laughs he phoned Charlie Benson, catching him as he was walking out the door.

"Mr. Benson, can you give me more information about a specific flight, like where it parked when it was here in Fort Lauderdale?"

"Which flight?" Benson asked, less than enthusiastically.

Bruce told him about the flight to Asheville and provided the tail number.

"And if you have it, I'd like to know where that plane parked after it landed in Asheville that night."

"Jesus, you're pushing it," Benson mumbled.

He put Bruce on hold for ten minutes.

"Okay," Benson said, back on the line. "On the date in question, that aircraft was parked over at Royal International. That's a company on the north side of the field here in Fort Lauderdale. I can't tell you where it parked when it got to Asheville that night."

"Why not?"

"Because that flight canceled its instrument flight plan twenty minutes before it was supposed to land in Asheville, and apparently went elsewhere."

Bruce wrinkled his nose.

"Is that unusual?"

"A bit, yes. He probably canceled IFR and made a visual landing at some other airport, which was allowed as long as he remained in radar contact."

"Why is that unusual?"

"Because," Benson said, "there's nothing but small Podunk airports outside of Asheville, certainly nothing big enough to handle a Boeing 737."

7.

The young man brazenly looked her up and down.

Rude son of a bitch, she thought.

"Hey, babe," he said with the confidence of a stud used to having his way with women. "You look like you know how to have some fun."

A surfer type with wild blond hair, wearing a T-shirt, bathing suit, and flops, he took the barstool next to hers.

In her younger days, she might have played along.

Now she just waved him off.

"Get lost," Tucker said coolly.

The third idiot to hit on her in the past ten minutes shrugged and got up. There would be plenty of other beautiful women to prey on here. This was the Fort Lauderdale Sands Resort, a ritzy, thousand-room hotel on the ocean, featuring an enormous pool area, including two bars. It drew a large meat-market crowd on weekends.

Despite being pestered, Tucker felt loose and easy as she sat under the shady overhang of one of the bars. It was a mellow Saturday afternoon, and her pina colada was cold. Steel drum, Calypso music throbbed in the background, and the subtle aromas of Coppertone and ocean salt wafted through the air. Appropriately for the occasion, she wore tight, white, terrycloth shorts, a blue tank top, dark sunglasses, and sandals.

Which certainly gave her the appearance of being on the make. But she was actually on the job. She had agreed to meet Detective Carlos Pena here. He had called the previous evening, saying he wanted to clear the air after their less-than-amicable parting at the police station.

Savvy and street-smart, Tucker figured Pena's real mission would be to rip into her—because her last column had made both the Police Department and Jim Norman look bad. If so, she would be ready. She knew how to work men like Carlos Pena, whether they were pissed at her or not.

She sipped her pina colada and saw that the surfer already had taken a lounge chair next to a bikini. But now three of his buddies were glancing at her, and she knew one of them would eventually wander over, which meant another tedious come-on.

Ah well, she thought. It still beat spending the day on the yacht with tiresome husband Bob. He had made plans for a day trip to Bimini, then had worn that pathetic hangdog look when she told him she had to work.

"Been waiting long?"

She turned to see Detective Carlos Pena. He wore a green Hawaiian shirt and khaki shorts, revealing sinewy arms and muscular legs. His facial skin

The East Side of Lauderdale

glistened from a recent shave and he smelled of sweet, subtle cologne.

"Detective," she said a bit too formally, though locked into his warm brown eyes. "Good to see you again."

He sat next to her.

"Please. Call me Carlos. It is Saturday, after all."

"Carlos, then."

He caught the attention of a bartender and ordered a light beer.

"This place is awesome," he said, looking around at the giant pool area.

"Yes, it certainly is. Why are we here again, Carlos?"

The standoffish tone was still in place. Pena took a breath.

"Sheryl, I want to apologize for that information leak to The Tattler."

"It was more like a gusher, Carlos. That pitiful little paper made me look silly, at least for a day."

"Look. I don't know how that happened. But I intend to find out and make sure it doesn't happen again."

"That would be nice."

"I'm trying to make amends here, Sheryl. And that is despite the fact I got my butt kicked because of your column yesterday."

Here we go, she thought.

"How so?"

"My lieutenant was ticked because it looked like we were withholding some sort of secret from the public. And Jim Norman complained that it looked like he was hiding something, too."

"Well, isn't he?"

His beer arrived and Pena took a swig.

"No, he isn't. He was silent on the matter at our suggestion. We advised him that we didn't feel the need to make a big splash about his wife missing, that we might be better off working this thing quietly."

"So, is Jim Norman coming after me now?"

"I doubt it. He's smart enough to know that if he makes waves, he's only going to end up looking bad all over again. In your column."

She smiled with contentment, a movie-star smile.

"In that case, your apology is accepted. But if you really want to make amends, you could keep me posted, step-by-step, of what's going on."

He took another sip of beer. She saw him glance at her legs.

"Sheryl, you know that I can't jeopardize the investigation. But I respect your work as a journalist and I can feed you a tidbit here and there."

She raised an eyebrow and sipped her pina colada.

"Have anything for me today, Carlos?"

"Actually, I do."

*

As she grabbed a notebook and pen from her purse, one of her admirers moseyed over. This one was even more muscular than the last guy, though his face was sunburned and his long, unruly hair was matted down from swimming. His words were slightly slurred from too much beer.

"Hey, gorgeous, this Julio bothering you?" He glared at Pena.

The East Side of Lauderdale

Pena and Tucker glanced at each other with some mirth. Both guessed he was a college kid, and the Ohio State T-shirt all but confirmed it.

When Pena refused to acknowledge his existence, the kid shoved him with a hand to the chest, hard enough that Pena had to catch his balance to avoid falling off the stool.

"You asshole Julio, you think that's funny?" the kid snarled. "You think I'm messing around?"

"Jesus," Tucker muttered, noticing heads around the pool area turn in their direction. "Testosterone. It should be an illegal substance."

Pena grimaced at her, still ignoring the kid.

"Give me a break, Sheryl. I'm not looking to mix things up. This punk's the one that's got his balls in an uproar. I'm just trying to have a quiet drink here."

The kid raised his fists.

"Listen, you greasy spic, I think the lady wants you to get lost so that me and her can have a private conversation."

When Pena finally turned to look at him, the kid tried to slug him. Displaying the quickness of a man who knew how to scrap, Pena easily dodged the fist. He jumped up, grabbed the kid's right arm and twisted it behind his back. Then he marched the kid to the pool, where, despite dozens of hotel guests looking on, he forced him to buckle to his knees. He grabbed a fistful of the kid's hair and dunked his head in the water, keeping it submerged for several seconds. When he let up, the kid was coughing and gasping for air. After Pena whispered some words in his ear, the young man vigorously nodded. Only then was he released.

Pena returned to his barstool next to Tucker while the kid limped back to his buddies. It was clear none of them wanted anything to do with Pena, even in defense of their friend.

"I'm sorry about that. But I think he has new respect for us Julios," Pena said nonchalantly. "Now where were we?"

Tucker eyed him, clearly impressed. The man was unflappable and quietly powerful, and that was undeniably appealing to her.

"You were going to give me something on the Melinda Norman case," she said, trying to match his calm.

"Ah yes," he said. "As of yesterday, we linked the Norman disappearance with three other women, all reported missing in the past six months."

Her eyes opened wide.

"Three others? Linked? How?"

"We have several common denominators. For starters, all resided on the East Side of town in well-to-do neighborhoods. All were businesswomen, holding responsible jobs or running their own companies. All were last seen after they left work. All were mothers. And all were in their mid-to-late thirties."

Tucker quietly whistled.

"Was there any press coverage when the other women went missing?"

"There was, but their cases died down before we could connect the dots."

"Why was that?"

"Mainly because we have dozens of missing persons cases, and frequently they resolve themselves. In just

The East Side of Lauderdale

the past few months, we have had at least seven spouses reported missing. In five of the cases, husbands just up and left. In two of them, wives ran off with lovers."

Tucker sipped her drink, thinking.

"How did you connect Melinda Norman with the other women?"

"After she was reported missing last week, we took the details of her case and ran it through the Florida Department of Law Enforcement's crime database. We found the MO in her case matched those of the other missing women. To make sure we haven't overlooked other possible abductions, we have formed a task force that consists of detectives from Fort Lauderdale, the Broward Sheriff's Office and the Florida Department of Law Enforcement."

When she finished scribbling, Tucker rested a hand on his arm.

"I appreciate this, Carlos. Now how about giving me the names of the other women? And the dates that they were reported missing?"

*

An hour later, Tucker was back in her office, all but hyperventilating.

"Richard! Get in here!"

Richard Bloom was quiet for a moment. This time he wasn't in the next office but rather in his seaside, high-rise condo five miles away, trying to enjoy a rare afternoon off with a good book and Vodka on ice.

"Sheryl," he said with tolerance, "this is Saturday. God said we rest on Saturday."

"That's only if you're a Jew, Richard."

"I am a Jew, Sheryl."

"You are not going to believe what I got. Four of them, Richard. Four!"

"Four what?"

"Four missing women! The cops linked the Melinda Norman abduction to three other women who they also think were abducted. It's incredible!"

"Four abductions? By the same person?"

"Or persons. So get your ass in here, pronto."

Bloom sighed. Sheryl Tucker was spoiled. She expected him, needed him, really, to hold her hand, even on a weekend. He took a long sip of Vodka and crunched on the ice, knowing she was waiting for an answer.

"Give me some time to clean up," he said.

Bloom arrived forty-five minutes later. Tucker was in her office with a phone headset on, furiously typing notes into her computer. She winked at him and he half-heartedly waved back. After settling into his office, he called the copy desk chief to suggest Tucker's column go on the front page. Then he punched up a solitaire game. It was going to be another late night.

*

She was between calls when her phone rang. She figured it was either Pena, trying to flirt a bit more, or her loathsome husband, trying to grovel a bit more. Hoping it was the former, she picked up.

"Sheryl, dear. How are you?"

It was Bradley Crawford, the retired federal judge, one of her breakfast buddies, checking up on her like a

The East Side of Lauderdale

father would a daughter. She muttered under her breath, resenting the disruption.

"Hello, Brad. I'm fine and I'm busy as hell."

"I figured as much. But I have another column idea, in case you're still in a jam."

"Actually, I'm not, and I'm on deadline."

"This will only take a moment. You might want to do something on all the Iraqis who live here in Florida, whether or not they have truly been accepted after all the—"

"Brad, that's a fabulous idea but we're going to have to discuss it another time. I really can't talk."

"Okay, sweetheart. If you need anything in the way of legal expertise, please feel free to call."

"Thanks. Love you, Bradley," she said, slamming the phone down. She loved having breakfast with Crawford and the other the older gentlemen, but she hated it when they called while she was working, and on a Saturday no less.

An hour later, she plopped down in a chair next to Bloom's desk.

"Okay. I talked to the families of the other three missing women. Two of the husbands gave me lots of details. The third was a bit hesitant but gave me enough to run with."

"Tell me about them," Bloom said.

"The first one abducted, about six months ago in early May, was Mary Sims. She owns a chain of clothing stores between Miami and West Palm. Mother of four, big in Chamber of Commerce circles and a self-made millionaire."

"Mary Sims," Bloom said, making a mental note.

"Then there's Charlotte Baker, marketing director for a high-end developer, abducted about a month later in June. She's reputed for being a rainmaker and pulls down a top salary. Lives in an exclusive condo on the beach, married to a successful attorney and has one child."

"She black?"

"The only one of the four who is."

"The third?"

"Janice Weslowski. President of an electronics firm that produces high-end video equipment, such as cameras and DVDs. Abducted in August after working late one night."

"And Janice, too, is a millionaire and a mother?"

"Twin daughters and a yacht."

"Geesh."

"Richard, this is going to blow the cork off this town. It's like we got a serial killer on the loose and we don't even know whether any of the women are dead."

Bloom nodded and looked at his watch.

"You'd best start writing, princess. Deadline is only seven hours away."

"Okay. I'm moving."

She started to walk away but turned around. She gave him a halfway-tender look, as though she was going to say something personal. He waited somewhat anxiously for her to get it out.

"Richard, if you would, order me a corned beef on rye and a diet cream soda from the deli. I didn't have much of a lunch."

Bloom sighed and nodded.

The East Side of Lauderdale

*

After the column was turned into the copy desk, Tucker and Bloom shut down their respective computers, locked their offices and walked to the parking garage. It was approaching midnight, and both were exhausted. He accompanied her to her car.

"Good night, Sheryl. Good work, as always."

Suddenly, she had that look again. She came close and gave him a quick peck on the lips.

"Thanks for being here, Richard. I don't know what I'd do without you."

Speechless, he watched her get into her Porsche, fire it up, and motor down the ramp toward the exit. He hopped into an eighteen-year-old Saab, still in mint condition, and drove slowly back to his condo. Once inside, he opened a sliding door to let the breeze flow into his fourteenth-floor perch. He put Brahms on the CD player and poured some Vodka on ice. Then he turned out the lights and collapsed in a recliner in his living room. In pleasant darkness, he listened to the music, sipped his drink and enjoyed the sea breeze.

And he thought about Sheryl Tucker's kiss long into the night.

8.

The blue Volkswagen Beetle pulled off to the side of A1A, just north of Las Olas Boulevard, its lights piercing the predawn gray. During the day, this was a bustling tourist area. Now it was still and quiet.

Bruce killed the engine and left the car haphazardly parked. Wearing blue jeans and a pullover shirt, he trudged to high-tide line and fell on the sand, throwing down the newspaper. Numbly, he sat and watched whitecap waves crash to shore for an hour, while the eastern sky turned shades of pink. A freighter floated motionless on the horizon, waiting to enter Port Everglades.

Eventually, he picked up the *Fort Lauderdale Post* from the sand and gazed once again at Sheryl Tucker's column. How in the hell did she discover that three other women were missing and connected to the Norman abduction?

In a flash of anger, he balled up the newspaper and threw it into the surf. For the second time in two days he had been journalistically bludgeoned on a story that

The East Side of Lauderdale

had become critically important to him. Initially, he wasn't quite sure why that was, but now it was clear. This was his shot at redemption.

Bruce closed his eyes and remembered how, just five months earlier in Dallas, he had cleaned out his desk, while the newsroom looked on with sadistic mirth. He had wanted to give up on his newspaper career in that dark moment.

But in the following weeks of introspection and gut-wrenching self-pity, he had come to realize that to quit was to be a loser.

And he never wanted to concede to being that.

Maybe it was his imagination, but it seemed like the freighter started to move. He stood, brushed the sand off his jeans and wandered back to his car.

Suddenly, he was famished.

*

After consuming a stack of pancakes and two cups of strong black coffee at a Denny's on Commercial Boulevard, he returned to the *Tattler* and punched on his computer. The sun was up, bright and streaming through the newsroom blinds. He was grateful that it was Sunday and the place was empty. His first task would be to verify the information in Tucker's column and hope that it contained gaps or errors. From there he would try to find a fresh angle.

But before he could make the first call, he found himself thinking about Officer Kasey Martin. He wondered if she, too, knew how it felt to be against the wall. At first blush he thought, no, she was too hard and focused. But then, maybe she did. She was flying nights yet wanted to be more involved in detective work. She seemed rather frustrated overall.

Curiosity got the better of him. He conducted an Internet search, cross-referencing her name and news stories involving the Fort Lauderdale police. He got four hits and, upon scanning them, sat back in disbelief. He had been right.

Seven months earlier, she had been flying a police helicopter above a tense hostage situation in southwest Fort Lauderdale. Her job was to provide surveillance to the SWAT team, which had surrounded an apartment complex in a quiet neighborhood. She was to radio in if she saw anything unusual.

As the team of heavily armed officers prepared to storm the building, the perpetrator suddenly appeared on the roof with an Uzi, holding the arm of a small gray-haired woman. But Officer Martin failed to immediately report this. For whatever reason, it initially appeared to her that the man was helping the woman take a walk, two people in the wrong place and time, and she never did see the Uzi. She took several seconds to study their movements before realizing the man was dragging the old woman against her will to the roof's edge.

By the time she radioed in, it was too late. She had left the officers on the ground vulnerable. The gunman sprayed the SWAT team as it rammed down a ground-level door. One officer was killed and two others seriously injured. When police returned fire, the deranged man blew away the old woman, who turned out to be his mother. Then he turned the automatic weapon on himself.

The East Side of Lauderdale

In the aftermath, the police Internal Affairs Division cleared Officer Martin of wrongdoing, at least from a legal standpoint. Yet she was cited for making an egregious error in judgment and relieved of active duty. Family members of the dead officer demanded that she be fired. But instead, she was quietly relegated to the lowly task of a nightly community air patrol.

Bruce drummed his fingers on his desk. Now he knew: Kasey Martin had a troubled past much as he did. Only in her case, the stakes had been much higher. She could have prevented a fellow officer from being killed.

He tried to imagine her pain and guilt and wondered if that, in some way, had led her to feed him the information about Melinda Norman.

*

Bruce's profile of Betty Sue Curtis, the local cable television woman, dominated the top half the East Lauderdale Tattler's Society Page on Monday morning. It included a large, complimentary photo of Betty Sue in her studio.

Seeing this, Bruce winced. It reminded him that not long ago he had covered the crash of a Lockheed L-1011 airliner at the Dallas-Fort Worth airport, killing more than a hundred people. He had won high praise for detailed and sophisticated coverage. Now he was writing soft features about home shopping network hosts.

"Jeff, could I see you, please?"

It was Sam, his editor, standing at the door to her office, dressed in an elegant beige pantsuit. There was an edge to her voice. This is where the going gets tough, he thought as he walked past her and into her glass office. She closed the door so hard that it was almost a slam.

"Sit down," she said, unmistakably irritated. She settled into the high-backed chair behind her desk. "Where were we with the three missing women?"

Bruce sat in a comfy, padded chair in front of her. Her desktop was neat and uncluttered. Two paintings of idyllic landscapes hung on crisp white walls. A five-iron golf club stood in a corner, a reminder that the *Tattler* was a half-step away from being a country club newsletter.

He wrinkled his nose as he thought of the diplomatic answer.

"Don't do that thing with your nose," she scolded. "It makes you look like a monkey."

"I don't have any excuses, Sam. I got beat."

"You got your ass whipped."

"I'm aware of that, Sam. What do you want me—?"

"I want you to catch up."

Though he didn't mean to, he wrinkled his nose again. This was strange. She had clearly warned that if he couldn't keep pace with the *Post,* then he would have to leave Melinda Norman behind and stick strictly to features.

"You're not taking me off the story?"

"No."

"But I thought you said—"

"Jeff, if you read the *Post* story you can see that all the victims resided in our backyard. They were high-profile businesswomen. Thus, this is an extremely important story to our readers. As a result, your priorities have been rearranged."

"But you said if I got beat again—"

"And now I'm saying drop everything else. Jump on this story with both feet. I do not want to see Sheryl Tucker embarrass us again. Are we clear?"

"You want me to jump on this with both feet," he repeated.

"Yes."

He hiked his shoulders.

"I actually started working on a follow-up yesterday and made a little progress. But it was Sunday and—"

"And today is Monday, when everyone should be available to answer your questions. I expect a strong story by the end of the day. Now leave me alone. I have things to do."

He got up slowly, pondering her change of direction. But it quickly dawned on him. Joe Petruska, the *Tattler's* publisher, probably saw Tucker's column and ordered Sam to assign someone to the abduction story full time. And Bruce was the only reporter who had the experience to handle it.

"I'm all over it, chief," he said, leaving her office.

*

Rather than wait for Detective Carlos Pena to return his calls, Bruce drove to the Fort Lauderdale Police Department. After waiting a half an hour, he was directed to the second floor. Pena, wearing a shoulder holster over a sports shirt, pointed to a folding chair on the side of his desk. He offered no handshake.

"I'm pressed for time," Pena said as Bruce sat down, "so make this quick."

"I'm wondering if you can give me the same police reports, photos and insight that you provided the *Fort Lauderdale Post*," Bruce said calmly.

Shuffling paper, the detective spoke without looking up.

"What newspaper did you say you're with again?"

"The *East Lauderdale Tattler*."

"That's like a shopper?"

Bruce knew that Pena was intentionally trying to piss him off.

"It's a small paper, yes. But it's delivered to nine thousand of the city's most prominent citizens, including City Commissioners, the Mayor and even the Chief of Police. I'm surprised you never heard of it. But then maybe you don't get over to the East Side of town very often."

Pena looked up abruptly, impatiently.

"I told you, I'm busy. So, no, I can't give you any of that information. It's all part of an official police investigation and closed to the public."

"I see," Bruce said, expecting that answer. "So you spoon-fed information to Sheryl Tucker because you only cooperate with pretty, female journalists?"

Pena narrowed his eyes.

"Listen, Mr.—"

"Bruce. Jeff Bruce."

"Listen, Mr. Jeff Bruce, Sheryl got that information from other sources. You see, even if the police don't release anything official, good reporters manage to get

The East Side of Lauderdale

what they need. If you worked for a big paper, you'd know that."

Bruce nodded and got up, half-tempted to mention his stint in Dallas.

"Thanks for your time, Detective Pena. But you should know something: I intend to talk to a lot of people and look under a lot of rocks. If I happen to find something, I'll be sure to return the favor and pass along nothing."

Pena furrowed his brow.

"Careful, Mr. Bruce. You don't want to cross me."

"No, I guess I don't."

Bruce departed, and Pena shook his head.

Pena's partner, who had been in a nearby office, poked his head in.

"What was that about?" asked Detective Jed Peterson.

"Beats the hell out of me," Pena said.

*

By late-afternoon, Bruce put together a respectable story, following up on Tucker's column on the three additional missing women, having gleaned most of his facts by talking to the victims' friends and families. Then he left the newsroom without waiting for Sam to edit it.

He drove to Fort Lauderdale-Hollywood International Airport and pulled into the parking lot at Royal International. This was home base for the Boeing 737 private jet that had departed on the evening the Norman woman was allegedly abducted. The big plane was now parked in front of a cavernous hangar.

As sunlight drained out of the western sky, Bruce positioned the VW so that he had a good view of the ramp area, commencing a private stakeout. He intended to monitor the other planes that left that same night. But he was most interested in the Boeing because it was registered to a firm that provided only a post office box for an address. That firm being RTE, Inc.

A rolling stairway had been pushed up to the plane's open cabin door, allowing workers to come and go. Bruce figured they were cleaning, stocking and preparing for the next flight, possibly to Asheville, its destination on the night Melinda Norman vanished. He wondered if that was where all the women had been taken and whether they were still alive.

After twenty minutes of pure boredom, Bruce saw two men come out of the jet. Both were rather young and dressed in everyday street clothes, one tall and blond, the other stocky and dark-haired. Both had a clean, all-American look, and he wondered if they were pilots.

They took the stairway down to the ramp and walked in Bruce's direction, prompting him to lean down out of sight. As they got closer, he could hear a smattering of their conversation through his open car windows.

"She was hot …"

" … a good one, boy …"

" … can't wait for the next …"

The two continued though a security gate, into the lot where his car was parked. They stopped to continue chatting by a white cargo van.

Now Bruce could hear them clearly.

The East Side of Lauderdale

"Rest up, because we have another assignment coming up," one said.

"I hope she's got red hair," the other said, "where it counts."

They laughed and parted. One got in the van, and another got into a maroon Ford F-150 pickup next to it. The two vehicles sped out of the parking lot—but not before Bruce copied down both license plates.

# **9.**

The red Jeep Wrangler slid to a halt. Officer Kasey Martin hopped out and walked briskly toward the Fort Lauderdale police hangar. She was supposed to start her aerial patrol at nine o'clock and already was a few minutes late.

But she suddenly stopped, noticing the man leaning against a small car ten yards away. She put her left hand up to shield her eyes from the glare of the parking lot security lights, while her right carefully fell to her sidearm.

She squinted, saying nothing.

"Just me," Bruce said, putting up both hands. "Don't blow my brains out."

"Jim," she said with obvious relief, recognizing him.

He smiled sardonically and walked over.

"Actually, it's Jeff, Jeff Bruce, the guy who rode with you a week ago."

He gazed at her hand over her gun, and she relaxed.

The East Side of Lauderdale

"Sorry. Jeff. I'm a mush-brain. What are you doing here?"

"Wanted to share something related to the Melinda Norman case. Remember you told me that a parking ticket stub was found in her car?"

"Yes, I remember."

"I followed up on it."

"How so?"

"I found out that several private flights left Fort Lauderdale one to two hours after her car entered the garage that evening. She could have been forced onto any one of them. Several commercial flights also took off in the same time frame. But no way was she forced onto an airliner, what with security."

Kasey tilted her head, allowing her thick dark hair to fall over one eye.

"And there's a distinct possibility she wasn't on any flight," she said.

"True. But I had to make some suppositions. For starters I'm think she was put on a jet, not a smaller prop plane. A jet would have been more convenient for a high-class abduction."

"What makes you think it was high-class?"

"Because Melinda Norman and the other women were high-class."

"That supposition may or may not hold true."

"I know, but I had to start somewhere. In the past few days, I've been staking out three private jets that took off between eight and nine that night."

She raised an eyebrow, amused.

"You were staking them out? Observe anything interesting?"

"Routine maintenance and cleaning work. But one jet did catch my attention: an airliner converted into a private jet. A Boeing 737, in fact."

"Yes. So?"

"So, while I'm watching this plane, I overheard two men making reference to a woman. I think they were pilots."

"Can you be more specific as to what you heard?"

"Sexual references like, 'She was really hot,' or 'She couldn't get enough.' One of them also said something about an assignment."

"Which probably translates to nothing."

"Or might translate to a lot. In any case, I got their license plate numbers."

She looked at her watch impatiently. "What are you suggesting?"

"That with these plate numbers you can start a criminal background check on these two men. Who knows what you'll find."

She gently shook her head, a gesture of disbelief.

"Let me get this straight. On a hunch, you zero in on a private jet because it's big. Then because you hear some guys talk dirty, you think they're suspects?"

He nodded. "That about sums it up."

She giggled but stopped when she saw his face remain rigid.

"Listen, Jeff, I was supposed to be up in the air five minutes ago. So I can't talk. All I can tell you is that, again, I'm not directly involved in the investigation. So even if you're onto something, it wouldn't be appropriate for me to—"

The East Side of Lauderdale

"Officer Martin, if you don't follow up on this, no one will. Detective Pena made it quite clear he has no use for me. I admit that I'm trying to pull a news story together. But I also think getting a read on these guys couldn't hurt from the police point of view."

He leafed through his notebook, found the page with the license plate numbers of the white van and maroon pickup, ripped it out, and handed it to her.

She took it hesitantly.

"I'll see what I can do. But I make no promises."

Bruce nodded.

"Thanks." Then he dug through his wallet and gave her a business card. "If you find anything, maybe you could call me."

He turned toward his car, holding up a hand to say goodbye.

He was almost to the VW when she called out.

"Jeff? Would you like to meet for a drink when I get down?"

*

It was almost midnight when they met at the Cloud Nine Pub on Commercial Boulevard, not far from Executive Airport. A dim, ordinary joint, lost in the neon lights of a strip shopping center, the bar had a couple of pool tables and a single television tuned to a college football game.

They found a booth in the back and ordered bottles of beer.

She asked, "So, what did you do for three hours?"

"Grabbed dinner. Took a walk. How about you?"

She sighed. "Flew around in circles, bored out of my gourd."

Their beers arrived and Bruce took a sip. Kasey tilted her head back and chugged. She put the bottle down hard, and for a moment Bruce thought she was going to let out a belch.

"Tell me about yourself," she said.

"Now that's really boring."

"Come on. I want to know."

"Born and raised in Detroit, only child. My father was a doctor. My mom, well, she was just a mom. They sent me to an all-boys private school. Never made the cut for the varsity football team. But I was a star on the high school newspaper. I had my own column, in fact. Attended Northwestern, got a degree in journalism and that's where I've been ever since."

She swigged and regarded him.

"You married?"

"Divorced," he answered.

"Kids?"

"Nope."

"What did you write about in your high school column?"

He smiled.

"Strictly gossip. Who was dating whom; it was called 'Jiving with Jeff.'"

She burst out laughing.

"'Jiving with Jeff?' Wow. That's great. Well, let me ask this, Mr. 'Jiving-with-Jeff': With all that stakeout work you've been doing and all your intuition, did you ever think about becoming a police officer?"

The East Side of Lauderdale

He saw how she continued to smirk as she hoisted her beer again. He looked down and wrinkled his nose.

"Okay, so it was a little hokey of me to stake out those planes. But I was just following my instincts. I wasn't pretending to be a cop."

"I'm not making fun of you, Jeff. I'm honestly impressed that you took that little piece of information from the parking stub and ran with it."

"It wasn't rocket science."

"You seem to be a step ahead of our guys. I don't think they thought about checking private planes on the night Melinda Norman disappeared. You know, Jeff, you seem too seasoned to be working at a small paper."

"That's because I worked at a big newspaper in Dallas for almost two decades. Covered a lot of big stories. But, well, here I am."

"What happened? Fired?"

He nodded slowly.

"Something like that. How about you tell me about yourself."

She took another long swig, sensing he didn't like talking about his past.

"What would you like to know?"

He wanted to know how she felt after making her own mistake, resulting in a fellow cop being killed, and two others wounded during the SWAT operation. He wanted to know if she, like he, had an interest in Melinda Norman as her own attempt to atone for sins past. But, more than these things, he wanted know why she had asked him here.

"You told me before that you were an experienced helicopter pilot, then got into police work. Why was that, again?"

She drank more beer. In the dim light her skin seemed an even darker shade of brown and her eyes even more Asian. Could she be part Korean?

"Maybe I saw too many cop shows, where they find one piece of evidence and that leads to the next. I'm fascinated by how good police work can uncover horrible crimes. Maybe what I'm really into is good old-fashioned justice. Anyway, the funny thing is, I want to be a detective."

"Not so funny. It's good to have ambitions. What would it take for you to move over to the Detective Bureau?"

"First I have to finish up my stint with the Aviation Unit, and I figure I'm stuck there for at least another year. Then I'll put in for a transfer to street patrol. If I do well there, I wait for an opening and an opportunity."

She was gazing at her almost-empty bottle, momentarily lost in her thoughts, and he wondered if she truly was eligible for any kind of promotion, considering the hostage incident.

"You said your boyfriend is a detective," Bruce said, pulling her eyes to his. "He working any interesting cases?"

She nodded.

"Actually, he's one of the primaries on the Norman case."

"I didn't know that," he said, though he suspected as much.

The East Side of Lauderdale

"Well, he is. That's why I was able to give you information about the ticket stub and such. But not anymore; it's too risky."

Bruce put down his beer.

"What do you mean, too risky?"

"I mean that I got that information from Jed's desk while he wasn't looking. And now the department is looking for a leak."

"Listen, Officer Martin—"

"Call me Kasey," she said, loosened by the alcohol and the hour.

"—Kasey. If someone from the department asks me, I'm not going to say where I got my information. I'm not going to reveal you as my source, if you're worried about that."

"Oh, I trust you, Jeff. The thing is, if Jed finds out that I even gave you the time of day, he'll beat me senseless. That's why it's important you keep my name completely out of anything you do on the Melinda Norman case."

"He'll beat you senseless?"

"I exaggerate. Just an expression."

She took a last pull, got up, and tossed a five-dollar bill onto the table.

"Got to get going. Thanks for the company, Jeff."

He stood up, but she waved him back down.

"Stay and finish your beer. Good to see you again."

"Same here," he muttered as she walked towards the door.

*

All the while, a man had been seated at the bar, his head down, staring into his drink. But as Kasey walked past him, he whipped around and grabbed her arm.

She gasped. "Jed ..."

He didn't say a word. The agitated look was his only greeting. The grip on her arm tightened, and he marched her back to where Bruce was seated.

The moment he saw what was happening, Bruce stood up, filled with adrenaline. He could see from Kasey's face that she was in turmoil.

As they approached, Bruce looked as coldly as he could into the big man's eyes and said, "Let her go."

Jed Peterson shoved her down into the booth where she and Bruce had been sitting. Then, with a snake strike, he grabbed Bruce by the throat with one hand. Bruce immediately felt his larynx being crushed.

"What'd you say, you little fuck?"

"Jed!" Kasey yelled. "Let him go!"

He ignored her and squeezed tighter. Bruce started kicking his legs.

"This little fuck still want to get in your pants, Kase?"

"Let him go, please!"

She tried to stand up and help Bruce get untangled from Peterson's grip. But he shoved her back down again with his free hand.

"Did you let him, Kase? Get in your pants?"

Now Bruce was flailing his arms as the blood supply to his brain was dwindling. His face flushed red, then drained white.

The East Side of Lauderdale

"Dammit, you're hurting him!" Kasey screamed, jumping up again and hitting Peterson's arm with clenched fists.

He relented and shoved Bruce to the floor, where he landed hard on his hind end. Peterson leaned over and wagged a finger at him.

"Thought I told you to stay clear of her, didn't I, you little fuck!"

Bruce looked at him with glazed eyes, gasping for air.

"Guess I don't take orders that well," he wheezed.

Peterson slapped him, producing a resounding crack and stinging pain. The bartender and a few middle-aged men at the bar saw this, but none dared come to Bruce's defense. The detective was bigger than most linebackers.

"You're going to start taking orders or get hurt bad. I'm telling you again: Stay the hell away from her."

He stood up and looked at Kasey, who was huffing in indignation.

"We'd best go back to my place and discuss this," he said, grabbing her by the arm again and pulling her toward the entrance.

"You son of a bitch! Leave me alone!"

She swung hard into his upper chest, which merely made him smile.

"Come on, Kase. I'm in the mood."

Kasey dug her feet in and leaned back, but he just dragged her across the floor. The patrons, including some aging bikers, idly watched. Some smiled.

"Leave me alone!" she cried.

Ken Kaye

"Don't worry, sweetheart. I'm going to make everything right between us," Peterson said as he had her almost to the bar's front door.

"No, dammit!"

Suddenly, Bruce went flying into Peterson's blind side like a hockey player streaming across the ice. The forearm to the bridge of his nose caught Peterson by surprise, and he fell to the ground, releasing his grip on Kasey.

"The lady asked you to leave her alone," Bruce vented, then kicked him in the stomach as hard as he could. He followed up with a single punch to his chin. The back of the big man's head snapped back and rebounded against the floor.

He lay motionless.

Bruce looked up to see Kasey breathing hard, looking at him. The anger had drained quickly, replaced by desperation.

"Are you all right?" he asked.

But she didn't answer. Instead, she ran out the door.

Bruce leaned down, put two fingers to Peterson's throat, and found a strong, fast pulse. He knew it would be a matter of minutes before the big man came to. He threw some money on the table and went outside after Kasey.

He caught up with her just as she was starting her Jeep.

"Kasey, answer me: Are you all right?"

She was staring straight ahead, the long hair in disarray over her face. Then she turned slowly to look at him.

The East Side of Lauderdale

"I know you were trying to be a good guy and look out for me, but you don't know what you just did."

"I know what he deserved."

"Yeah? Now he's going to take it out on me and come gunning for you."

The tremor and volume in her voice revealed that she was legitimately terrified. Bruce took a chance and put a hand on her shoulder.

"Kasey, you need to get away from that weirdo. File stalker charges against the guy. Domestic violence charges. Something. Because I know you weren't exaggerating when you said he'd beat you senseless."

She reached over and harshly pushed away his hand. The wheels of her Jeep spun, kicking up dust, and she peeled out of the parking lot.

Bruce watched her go, inwardly decreeing that, henceforth, it would be best to stay clear of her—and Jed Peterson.

10.

Bob Tucker was in his den on Wednesday morning, organizing his desk. Organization, after all, was key to his incredible success. He was the head of a giant empire that included major real estate holdings throughout the United States and Europe, two lumber mills in Canada, a paper mill in Tennessee, a steel-production plant in Northeast Ohio, a concrete plant in Central Florida and numerous other highly lucrative concerns.

To run all these businesses, Tucker set up headquarters in his own thirty-floor high-rise in downtown Fort Lauderdale, where he usually worked only half a day, three days a week, on, of course, the thirtieth floor. There, in an office the size of a high school gym, he kept a desk just as neat and immaculate as the one at his home. He was a good manager who knew how to delegate, so most of his tasks simply involved looking over the shoulders of the many handsomely paid CEOs who oversaw the operations of his various industries.

Overall, Tucker was worth about three billion. Which wasn't bad, considering he had been raised dirt-

The East Side of Lauderdale

poor in the shadow of a car factory in Cleveland. But here he was, at the age of fifty-five, enjoying all the fruits of his labors, including the palatial home in Fort Lauderdale, a private jet, an ocean-going yacht, and a gorgeous wife to share it all with.

Now he was freshly showered and shaved, though he had no plans to visit his downtown office that day. He wore a dark-blue suit, white shirt and crimson tie, and his gray hair was neatly combed back. He wanted to look nice for his lovely young bride and perhaps catch her in a submissive mood—knowing full well that she would look delectable after primping for her day at work.

Much to his delight, she soon appeared in the doorway.

"I have to run, Bob. Have a nice day."

He gazed at her over the reading glasses resting on the end of his nose.

"Wait a minute, dear. Let's have a look at you."

Sheryl Tucker's head sagged. Dammit, she thought.

She walked closer so he could have a better view. He took off the glasses and softly whistled. She had squeezed into a red, sleeveless dress with a slit high up the thigh. It also was cut high above the knees and low on the chest. Her brushed-out hair cascaded over her shoulders.

"You look incredible," he whispered.

"Goodbye, Bob," she said intolerantly, knowing exactly what he wanted. "I really have to run."

"Wait a minute. Please."

He walked over and placed hands on her shoulders. Then he pulled her close. As she was slightly taller, her chin rested uneasily on his shoulder, so he couldn't see her nose crinkling at his overly powerful and sweet cologne.

"You know, it's been awhile since we've made love," he cooed in her ear.

His hands dropped down and started to hike the red dress up.

She pulled away angrily and pulled the dress down.

"Dammit, Bob, not now. Didn't you hear me? I have to go."

She stormed out of the den, grabbed her purse off a foyer table, and trotted toward the garage. She heard him call out, but she kept going.

"Will I see you tonight?" There was a pathetic quality to his voice.

"I doubt it."

A minute later, she backed the Porsche out so quickly that she almost ran into the garage door as it was opening. Then she wheeled around the large driveway and gunned it into the street.

Bob Tucker went to the window of his den, offering a nice view of his expansive front yard and the street, and solemnly watched her car disappear.

*

As she raced south on Federal Highway, Tucker couldn't let go of the nagging feeling that it was time to stop kidding herself. She wanted to believe that she and Bob had a real marriage and could find some semblance of contentment. But she knew that was far from true. In reality, she was deeply frustrated because there was no real emotional connection. She had wasted too much

The East Side of Lauderdale

time pretending to love him, and it was high time to seek a divorce. She and Bob had grown too far apart.

When she had first met him, she had been fresh out of college, boasting a Master's Degree from the prestigious Columbia School of Journalism, starting out as a rookie reporter for the *Fort Lauderdale Post*. She had been covering a political fund-raiser, and Bob Tucker was among the guests. They chatted and she found him intriguing. Though rather quiet, he seemed so worldly, what with a vast real estate and financial empire.

They quickly found they had at least one thing in common, and that was their meager beginnings. Like Bob, Sheryl Tucker, born Sheryl Nicodemus, had come from a working-class family, born to parents who had to claw their way through life. It was because she had been underprivileged as a child, growing up in a rundown section of Chicago, that she also had been driven to excel in college and journalism. She wanted to make her parents proud and forge to lofty places that no one in her family had ever been to.

Perhaps for these reasons, she saw stars in Bob Tucker, because at the time, he already had made it to the top. She envisioned a dignified life with a man of class and wealth. He might have been more than twenty years her senior, but he had social status and business connections and offered unlimited financial security. Though she wanted to be beholden to no one, she thought he could do nothing but help her climb the corporate ladder.

They were married within six months of that fundraiser and, indeed, her career took off like a shot.

Ken Kaye

She went from rookie reporter to general assignment reporter to the prestigious role of columnist all within a year. Despite some mean-spirited rumors—among them, that her husband frequently played golf with the *Post's* publisher—she never thought for a moment that Bob had anything to do with her meteoric rise, other than giving her an air of confidence. And, in truth, she had legitimately earned her spot at the top of the newsroom pecking order through hard work, long hours, and a lot of smarts.

But, while her career flourished, in time their marriage deflated. Each of their five years together became more boring than the previous one. Bob had no real interest in her work and she certainly had none in his. He wanted to laze on their yacht and attend dinner parties on weekends, while she preferred to work out in a gym and spend time in the newsroom, getting a jump on the workweek. Their sex life became a bit weird because he always wanted to couple at odd times, such as just before she went to work or the moment she returned home. If she denied him, he would punish her with long bouts of moodiness.

Now, as she aimed the Porsche through morning traffic, she realized she probably never really loved him and that she had made a horrible mistake assuming his social connections and business acumen would make her happy. She further wished that she had put more faith in herself to get through life without his bottomless bank accounts.

Thus, right in the middle of rush hour, she decided that as soon as this Melinda Norman episode came to a conclusion, she would end it with Bob. To do so sooner

The East Side of Lauderdale

would be a major distraction at a time when she needed focus. She would ask for a reasonable settlement, only a few hundred million or so. It would be enough that she could retire comfortably. Yet, for now, she would continue working because her column provided too much satisfaction.

As she continued maneuvering south, approaching the Southeast 17th Street Causeway, her cell phone rang. Her stomach tightened, as she feared it might be her prickly little husband making some sort of overture. She knew that her red dress would be on his mind all day long. She hesitantly answered.

"Sheryl, dear. How are you?"

She immediately recognized the voice of Clayton McGreggor, one of her breakfast buddies and one of South Florida's most prolific developers. At the moment she didn't want to talk to him or anyone else. But at least it wasn't Bob.

"In the biggest rush of my life, Clay. How are you?"

"Fine, fine. I'm here at the Floridian with the boys. We were wondering if you're going to join us today?"

"Sorry, I can't. I have another breakfast date."

"I'm crushed! We're going to miss you."

"Thanks, me, too," she said, lying and hoping to end the call quickly.

But no such luck.

"Sheryl, you had been searching for some column ideas. I wanted you to be the first to know that CM Limited, which is the architectural arm of my development firm, has submitted plans to build exact replicas of the twin World Trade Center towers, only on a smaller scale, on a vacant piece of land in Lighthouse Point. You know, the towers that were attacked by the terrorists—"

"Yes, Clayton, I'm familiar with the World Trade Center and September Eleventh. That's interesting but not my cup of tea. I'll let the editors know about it and maybe they'll have another reporter contact you."

"That would be fine, dear. I wanted to make sure you weren't without something to work with."

"Oh, I got plenty to work with, with this Melinda Norman thing."

"So I've seen. Anyway, if you want tickets to see the Bashers play this weekend, let me know." The Bashers were the football team McGreggor owned. They were part of yet another new league trying to compete with the NFL.

"Thanks, Clay. Right now I got plans."

"Okay, dear. Have a nice—"

But she already had hung up.

From the urban clutter of Federal Highway, she turned right on Griffin Road, a green-lined thoroughfare, at least as far as it ran through the East Side of town. Just short of Interstate 95, she turned into the Sheraton Hotel, which sat on the west edge of Fort Lauderdale-Hollywood International Airport. Planes actually made their final approaches right over the hotel's multi-level parking garage.

Inside, she made her way to the coffee shop, where Detective Carlos Pena was seated at a corner table. He stood up when he saw her.

"Sheryl," he said warmly. "Thanks so much for coming."

The East Side of Lauderdale

Somehow the man got better-looking each time she saw him. Today he reminded her of a young Al Pacino.

"Good to see you again, Carlos." She sat down and crossed her legs. "You said you had something important to pass along."

"Yes," he said. "An interesting development."

A waitress came by to fill Tucker's coffee cup, and both ordered scrambled eggs and dry toast. As soon as the waitress walked away, Pena leaned over the table and kept his voice low.

"We have linked one of the three women I told you about to one Frank Petrucco. That would be Janice Weslowski, who runs a company that manufactures video equipment. As it turns out, she was a business associate of his. A very close associate."

Tucker put down her cup and held up a hand.

"Whoa. Back up. Who the hell is Frank Petrucco?"

"You don't know Frank Petrucco?"

"I've never heard of Frank Petrucco."

Pena took a sip of his coffee.

"Petrucco is one of the most powerful organized-crime figures in the Southeast. He owns some hotels and restaurants. But his bread and butter is a large porno operation, including a studio and distribution warehouse. While that's not illegal, we think it's a front for racketeering activities."

"One of those."

"Yes, one of those. We've been watching him for some time, hoping he'll do something stupid. But so far he hasn't."

Tucker thought a moment.

"So you think, because this guy Petrucco was connected to one of the abducted women, that he's your guy? How was he connected?"

Before Pena could answer, the waitress delivered their breakfasts, and both dug in. After a few bites, Pena dabbed his mouth with a napkin.

"We think Janice Weslowski was having an affair with Petrucco, even though he's supposedly happily married—to a young, beautiful woman, I might add. Weslowski has been separated from her husband for some time now. So we think she might have been putting pressure on Petrucco to leave his wife. She might have been threatening to reveal the affair. For a man of his stature, that would be highly embarrassing, not to mention, he'd probably lose the wife."

"How did you learn of this alleged affair?"

"Her jilted husband found some sort of love note from Petrucco hidden in a drawer. He had been going through her things after she was reported missing."

"Did Janice Weslowski and Frank Petrucco actually have a business relationship, or were they just lovers?"

"As we understand it, her company sold him a large quantity of professional video cameras and high-quality production equipment, which he used to make porn. Whether Weslowski knew this is unknown."

Tucker nibbled on a piece of toast.

"Is Petrucco linked to any of the other women who were abducted?"

"Not that we know of," he said. "We have no theories on why he might want to abduct or kill the other women. We only know that he could have motive to do harm to Janice Weslowski."

The East Side of Lauderdale

"Is Frank Petrucco then the prime suspect?"

"Let's just call him a 'person of interest' for now."

Tucker was quiet for a long moment, staring at her plate, then she looked up.

"Carlos, once again, I thank you for you giving me this."

She thought she saw the detective blush.

"We think very highly of you, Sheryl."

"We?"

"The Department. And, well, me. I think very highly of you."

She smiled demurely and shoveled some eggs in her mouth.

The red dress had paid off.

*

By mid-afternoon, Tucker turned in a column on how a reputed mobster named Frank Petrucco was connected to at least one of the four women suspected of being abducted by the same person or persons.

She rested on a couch in Richard Bloom's office as he read through the column, his eyes darting back and forth across his computer screen.

He asked, "So, are we saying that this Petrucco is the prime suspect?"

She yawned.

"Nope. We're saying that the police think he was romantically involved with one of the women, and thus they have reason to believe he might be a suspect. For now the police are only calling him a person of interest."

"Then let's say that so we don't get our asses sued," Bloom said evenly. He tapped the keyboard, making an adjustment to her column.

"From what I understand, suing people isn't Frank Petrucco's style."

"What is?"

"Killing them."

"All the more reason to get his exact status correct. And since we don't directly quote any police officials, but rather rely on 'a reliable source,' may I assume this is your detective friend?"

"That's right."

Bloom knew it was verboten to use unnamed sources because of the perception that a journalist might be manufacturing information. But he trusted Tucker explicitly.

"Thought so."

Tucker stood up to return to her office. But then she turned and saw Bloom fixating on her tight, red dress. It was the same look she had seen on her husband and Carlos Pena earlier that day.

"What is it, Richard? Something wrong?"

He shook his head, unnerved at being caught gawking.

He almost stammered.

"Just ... just wanted to say another great column."

She smiled and walked out, thinking all men were alike: horny dogs.

Feeling tiny beads of sweat form on his forehead, Bloom loosened his tie, lowered his head and pinched the bridge of his nose. At that moment he wished he wasn't Sheryl Tucker's editor because it was becoming too difficult to be so close to her, knowing he could never have her.

11.

Betty Sue Curtis was dying for a glass of wine. After spending the day at her cable television studio, laboring as the popular host of a home shopping network show, she was at once wound-up and exhausted.

At thirty-eight, Betty Sue possessed earthy beauty. Unlike most television personalities who were overly primped, she let her long dirty blond hair fall lazily around her oval face and rarely wore makeup. Her wardrobe tended toward 1950s fashions, yellow summer dresses and white high heels. Though tall and graceful, she had a country girl manner.

"See this doodaddy? It'll only cost ya two-hundred and fifty smackeroos," she might say in a rural Alabama accent while selling a watch.

Her show consistently won high ratings based largely on her charisma. The *Fort Lauderdale Post's* television reviewer once gushed that she was a cross between Dolly Parton and Faith Hill. The *Miami Journal* proclaimed her Southern style "refreshing for

The East Side of Lauderdale

the home-shopping genre." And only a few days earlier the *East Lauderdale Tattler* had featured her on its Society Page.

Now Betty Sue walked across the parking lot behind the studio as a trickle of burnt-orange light remained on the western horizon. She hopped into a Mercedes convertible, silver with a black top, and tuned the radio to a classical station. She looked forward to dining with her husband and their three children at an Italian restaurant near their home on the East Side of Fort Lauderdale. There, she could finally have a glass of wine, maybe two.

But, as she drove out of a well-lit parking lot onto the studio's dark access road, two pairs of headlights suddenly appeared. A white Ford Econoline van pulled along side her, and a maroon Ford pickup made its way in front. They boxed her in, slowed her down, and forced her to the side of the access road.

The moment she realized what was happening, Betty Sue Curtis felt a shot of primal fear in the pit of her stomach. But she didn't panic. She had grabbed her cell phone from her purse and called 911 even before they got her stopped.

"What is that nature of your emergency?"

"Two vehicles forced me off the goddamn road," Betty Sue all-but-shouted.

"Okay, but you're calling on a mobile, so we can't get a lock on your location, ma'am. Can you tell me where you are, exactly?"

"A side road off Stirling. Damn. What's the name? Runs right to my studio, which is—"

Just then, the passenger side window exploded. The glass shattered and some of it fell in Betty Sue's lap. A man stood next to her car with a crowbar in his hand. He had a marine crewcut and was built like a stocky football player.

"Ma'am? Ma'am?" the dispatcher inquired.

Betty Sue was so dumbfounded that she didn't scream for help. The man jumped in beside her. Wearing a black short-sleeve shirt and black leather gloves, he snatched the phone out of her hand and threw it out the window.

"Follow the van. Keep your mouth shut and do exactly as I tell you or else I'm going to jam the business end of this crowbar in your ear," he said.

*

As she followed the van west on Stirling Road, Betty Sue stared straight ahead, jaw tight. A cool wind flowing in from the busted-out window chilled the sweat beading on her forehead. She tried to get a read on the young man beside her. He displayed an icy calm for someone who had just committed a felony carjacking. She sensed it would irk him if she tried to talk to him.

So she kept her mouth shut.

Where they were going didn't concern her so much as why. She figured this man and his partner in the van would attempt to rape her in a remote location. Then they probably would kill her because she had seen their faces.

Betty Sue Curtis quickly formulated other plans.

The East Side of Lauderdale

Despite the country girl exterior, she was a fighter who knew how to defend herself. She had her father to thank for that. He had been a Marine lieutenant who survived two tours in Vietnam. While she was still in grade school, he had taught her hand-to-hand combat skills at a black-belt level.

The tomboy in her took advantage of this. In junior high, she had pummeled a boy who stuck a tack on her desk chair. In college, she almost knocked out a guy who he wouldn't take no for an answer. As an adult, she regularly worked out to stay proficient in attack, counter-attack routines.

Her father also had been a marksman and trained her in the use of firearms. He would let her squeeze off rounds from his Beretta M9 semiautomatic sidearm at gun ranges. Accordingly, once she was old enough, she obtained a special permit for a snub-nose .38, which she now kept in the glove compartment of her Mercedes.

As she drove westward against her will, she remembered her father's rules when encountering a hostile situation. First: Stay calm. Second: Make a quick assessment of how to resolve the conflict. Third: Don't hesitate to act.

From the size of his biceps, she knew it would be dangerous to engage the gorilla beside her, at least in the small confines of her car. He was unquestionably powerful, and for all she knew, he might be a martial-arts expert as well. She needed the element of surprise.

Thus, she decided that when the moment was right, she would grab the .38 out of the glove compartment and blow his brains out. While she was at it, she would kill the partner in the Ford van if he were within firing range.

That would make Daddy proud.

Of course she would attempt to avoid the double-kill scenario if she saw a police car. In that event, she would cut in front of the cop to get his attention. That would bring a halt to this lunacy. Unfortunately, Stirling Road aimed into rural territory; horse farms, orange groves, and open fields; where the chances of finding an officer were slim.

So she concentrated on Plan A: The gun.

Twenty minutes later, the van slowed and turned onto a dark, side road.

"Keep following him," the man next to her said.

She nodded. But her heart quickened pace. This was far from civilization, and she was sure they would soon make their move against her.

The time to ice this creep was drawing near.

*

After gliding a half a mile down the darkened road, the van pulled off onto a small dirt trail. She could see no homes in the vicinity.

"Pull up beside him."

She did so, to the van's passenger side.

"Now, ma'am," the crewcut said in a soft, southern accent, not nearly as thick as hers, "here's what we're gonna to do. You're going to get out of this car nice and easy and get into that van. You run, you're going to piss me off to no end. We understand each other?"

She nodded.

The East Side of Lauderdale

The Ford Econoline left its motor running, dust clouding up in its headlights. The driver hopped out. He was carrying something shiny that reflected light. She gasped when she realized it was chains and handcuffs. But she retained her steely composure, knowing she would need it to come out of this alive.

"Now turn off the engine and give me the keys," the crewcut said.

This was the make it or break it point. Either she put a bullet between this Neanderthal's eyes, or she ended up in those shackles.

She clicked the key off, killing the engine, and pulled it halfway out of the ignition switch. She turned to give the man nervous smile, a bit of distraction. He remained expressionless but kept his eyes locked on hers.

Then, in as fast and fluid a motion as she could muster, she lunged for the glove compartment and managed to flick the handle open. She fumbled for the gun and got a hand on it.

But he slammed a forearm into the side of her head and knocked her back against her door. He looked in the glove compartment, found the gun, and nonchalantly heaved it out the busted window. It landed in nearby bushes.

"Knew you were going to try something like that," he said without emotion.

Growling, she turned and tried to stab his neck with her knuckles, hoping to crush his windpipe. But he dodged the blow with catlike quickness and was able to latch onto both of her wrists.

"You're a feisty one," he groaned. "Brad, some help here!"

The other man opened her driver's side door, grabbed her under the arms and yanked her out of the vehicle.

"Sons of bitches!" she screamed, kicking and squirming.

Within seconds, the two men dragged her to the van and pulled her into its dark interior, where she was thrown onto her stomach. Her hands were cuffed behind her back, her feet were shackled, and duct tape was place over her mouth. For good measure, they threw a black hood over her head.

*

Trapped in the darkness of the hood, Betty Sue breathed deeply through her nose, the black material rising and falling against her nostrils. Despite fear and enormous stress, she inwardly vowed to remain cool, wait for another moment, and get through this ordeal.

She guessed they were driving east, probably to retrieve the pickup on the access road near her studio. She figured the trip west was intended to hide her Mercedes in a place that would take police days, if not weeks, to find it.

The question now was what were they going to do with her?

Soon the van came to a stop, and one of the men hopped out.

"See you there," she heard the crewcut say, then slam the van door shut.

The East Side of Lauderdale

The van drove off with Betty Sue Curtis still shackled in its darkened interior. A short while later, it came to a halt. From the whine of distant jet engines she knew they had come to an airport. The van's side door slid open. The two men pulled her out and dragged her across an asphalt surface.

They began to lead her up a grated-metal staircase, and Betty Sue instantly knew she was being taken onboard an aircraft. She suddenly stomped a white high heel onto the top of the shoe of the man to her right, prompting him to howl in pain, hop on his opposite foot and relax his grip on her.

"Mother fuck!" he yelped.

She ripped her left arm free from the other man and shuffled away as fast as she could with shackles around her ankles and a hood over her face.

It only took a second for the crewcut to catch her. He slapped her incredibly hard on the back of her head, and Betty Sue Curtis went limp.

"Bitch," he mumbled. "That really hurt, what you did to my foot."

The crewcut put one arm under her knees and the other around her back. He picked her up and carried her effortlessly up the stairway to the aircraft cabin, even though she weighed more than one-forty. He dropped her down in a seat and left without a word.

Five minutes later, the cabin door was closed and locked. The engines whined to life and the plane taxied toward its runway. Soon it throttled up and lifted off. Betty Sue felt the forces of gravity and despair grab at her very soul.

Yet she resolved, more than ever, to remain strong, to win this battle. That was what her father, the unflappable Marine, would want her to do. She closed her eyes under the hood and tried to reserve her strength. She also tried to forget about the throbbing pain on her head, where she had been smacked.

Ten minutes into the flight, there was a burst of light, as the crewcut lifted the hood, pulled the tape from her mouth, and unlocked the shackles.

"Make yourself at home," he said in that quiet, calm southern voice. "Bathroom's in back and coffee and sandwiches are in the galley."

She glared at him with raw anger but made no attempt to move on him, now very much aware of his strength. Seeing that he had obtained the upper hand, he smirked and shook his head. Then he disappeared into the cockpit.

She immediately ran to the rear lavatory to relieve her swollen bladder. When she came out, she took careful inventory of the cabin. It was big and laid out in a white décor with modern couches, comfy lounge chairs and a conference center with a TV and stereo. But in effect, it was a luxurious prison.

She retook her seat by a window, a gamut of emotions surging through her, starting with rage. But as the plane swam upward over a mat of city lights, she knew she had to keep her anger in check because it would hurt her ability to think rationally. She sensed that the worst was yet to come.

*

The East Side of Lauderdale

Two hours later, the plane made a steep approach into a dark, sparsely populated area. She could tell from the few runway lights that this was a private strip. The jetliner taxied to a ramp and shut down next to a lodge of some sort.

The two men escorted her down the plane's stairs, across the ramp and inside. She put up no resistance as they took her through a hotel-like lobby and up a flight of stairs to a spacious and neat bedroom.

"Make yourself at home," the crewcut said. "You'll find clean towels, toothbrushes, what have you, in the bathroom. There's some night things in the drawer. See you in the morning."

For the first time, Betty Sue Curtis looked into the eyes of her abductors and spoke directly to them.

"Why don't you boys," she stated flatly, "go fuck yourselves."

The two men glanced at each other and smiled.

*

After they were gone, Betty Sue explored every inch of her new prison. The door was locked from the outside. The windows opened but had steel bars outside of them. As she suspected, there was no way out.

Meandering into the bathroom, she gazed at the oversized bathtub and thought how good hot water would feel all over her body. But she resisted that urge, fearing they were spying on her with video cameras.

She returned to the bedroom, went through the drawers and indeed found several nighties. She checked the closet and saw that it was full of women's clothing. Taking a closer look, she noticed that the dresses were exactly like the ones she wore while on the studio set, and in her size. She immediately understood the implications. Someone had selected her specifically as a target.

She hunted for any kind of object that could be used to chisel her way through a wall, or as a weapon. But there was nothing. She paced and thought, reviewing every detail of her abduction and of her abductors, trying to assess where they might have weaknesses. At two in the morning she finally was overcome by exhaustion and passed out on the bed, never changing out of her clothes.

She awoke shortly before noon the next day, bounded up and discovered the door to her room was unlocked. But the moment she opened it, she heard the calm southern accent of the crewcut.

"Come on down. Have some lunch. You already missed breakfast."

She looked up to see the surveillance camera mounted in the hallway ceiling outside the bedroom door. They had been waiting for her to emerge. She still ran down the stairs, through the lobby and straight to the front door. She tried fervently to open it, only to find it was locked.

The two men sat in comfy chairs near a security console of video screens, watching her and chuckling. But they jumped up when they saw her grab a chair and try to swing it through the glass panes on either side of that door.

"Settle down, now," the goatee said. "Be a good girl."

The East Side of Lauderdale

Hair falling over her face, Betty Sue Curtis spat at him.

"Bitch," the goatee said, drawing back his arm to backhand her.

"Brad!" crewcut yelled. "Don't hurt the merchandise."

The goatee caught himself.

"Take her back to her room, Ray," he said in a restrained voice. "Let her starve."

She gave the goatee the finger then trudged up the stairs with Ray, the crewcut, who clung to her upper arm. After he locked her in the room, she sat on the bed and fought off every urge to cry and go soft. She forced herself to keep thinking of ways she might foil the men, break away. She had to find some kind of opening, as she desperately wanted to survive this and see her husband and children again.

Yet an hour later, she was powerless to stop them from coming into her room and peeling her out of her rumpled clothing, their big video camera set up to capture every detail of their assault and her screaming and struggling.

"Daddy!" she cried.

12.

For three days Bruce tried to follow Tucker's column on how organized crime figure Frank Petrucco was linked to the missing women. He did so with little success. Despite Petrucco's high profile in law enforcement circles, few of Bruce's sources had even heard of him.

Bruce hadn't either. Even after drawing on Internet databases, he was unable to obtain a clear picture of the man. Which made it obvious that someone had again spoon-fed extremely sensitive information to Tucker.

Amazingly, his snippy young boss, Samantha Pauline VanDermark, understood his predicament and put no undue pressure on him to come up with a story replicating Tucker's column. Yet Bruce insisted on getting on record with the organized-crime angle, even though he was tired of chasing the competition.

Thus, on a Thursday evening, after most of the *Tattler's* newsroom had cleared out, Bruce called the FBI's local racketeering task force, hoping to get a

The East Side of Lauderdale

handle on Frank Petrucco. An agent who refused to give his name answered.

"You want me to confirm what?"

"That you guys are looking at Frank Petrucco as a suspect in the disappearance of the four women, that supposedly he was having an affair with one of them," Bruce said patiently.

The man rudely chuckled.

"You media guys. You kill me. You think I'm going to tell you who we're looking at so you can broadcast it to the world and screw up our investigation? Listen. Let's skip Petrucco and go straight to the Kennedy assassination. I'll fill you in on the second gunman. That work for you?"

Bruce ignored the sarcasm.

"Someone who didn't give a rat's rear-end about your investigation has already unloaded Petrucco's whole case file on the *Fort Lauderdale Post*. I'm just looking to get the same information from another direction."

"Well, you're not the *Post*, are you?"

Then came more cruel laughter followed by the man hanging up without the courtesy of a goodbye. Bruce slumped in his seat, knowing that the FBI probably was his last hope of catching up to Tucker. Now he would have to accept the unsavory prospect that it was time to put aside the story on the abductions and return to junky little features.

He shook his head and grabbed his car keys. He needed a drink.

Rush hour was still a mad stampede as he aimed his Volkswagen east on Commercial Boulevard and into another cool evening. He crossed over the Intracoastal Waterway and turned into a trendy area of waterside bars and restaurants. He parked in front of a popular sports lounge called the Busted Bat, knowing it had televisions tuned to most every game in the nation that night. For whatever reason, he had a hankering to see his hometown Detroit Pistons play some hoops.

Although the place was hopping, he found several open barstools in front of a set tuned to the Pistons-Lakers game. The air was filled with the aromas of beer, peanuts, and grilling hamburgers.

"What'll it be?" a bored, graybeard bartender asked.

"Dewars, rocks."

As he watched the bartender grab a bottle and pour the scotch over ice, he was heartened that he had come here. The jovial, yet casual, atmosphere was a good diversion from the stress. When the drink arrived, he took a sip and further relaxed. The alcohol felt warm and good in his stomach.

He watched a player on television make a perfect jump-shot and suddenly thought of her beautiful form on the courts at the beach. He took another sip and wondered where Kasey was that night. Probably with that brute-cop boyfriend, he figured, and somewhere deep down that hurt. After that scene at the bar near the airport, he realized the chances of connecting with her again were remote.

In another section of the cavernous lounge, a cluster of Miami Heat fans let out a roar, prompting Bruce to crane his neck in their direction. When he turned back, a woman was nonchalantly taking the barstool next to his. Considering all the empty stools nearby, he found

The East Side of Lauderdale

this interesting. He managed to give her a tired smile as a greeting.

"How ya doing, partner," she said in the husky voice of a smoker, who wasn't allowed to smoke, even in a bar, under Florida law.

There wasn't anything remarkable about her. She seemed to be in her late thirties and had blond hair that was obviously dyed. She wore pearls around her neck, a black blouse and an off-white skirt. Her fingernails were painted blood-red and she reeked of cheap perfume. Bruce guessed she was a secretary who shied away from the meat-market scene, preferring a less-competitive sports bar.

"I'm doing all right," he said and returned to the Pistons game.

"You look a little lonely," she boldly observed. "Buy a girl a drink?"

Bruce raised his eyebrows and shrugged.

"Yeah, sure."

He called over the bartender and the woman ordered a gin and tonic.

"Linda," she said, extending a hand.

"Jeff," he said, shaking it, now thinking that maybe she was a car salesman. This was how they got to you, getting on a first-name basis. Probably sells Hondas or Fords because she wasn't the BMW or Jaguar type, he thought.

Her drink was placed on a cocktail napkin and she sipped through the little straw. He noticed a smudge of lipstick at the corner of her mouth.

"So what do you do, Jeff?"

He was about to answer honestly when a touch of paranoia seeped in. For all he knew, Frank Petrucco had dispatched this woman to get a read on him, find out why he had been making inquiries.

"I'm a pilot for Delta Air Lines," Bruce said, studying her to see if the lie registered any surprise. But she appeared to take him at face value.

"Fly those big jets, eh? I'll bet it gets boring up there in the cockpit, just watching clouds go by."

"Well, you know what they say about flying, hours of boredom interspersed with moments of terror."

She slurped her drink and eyed him.

"You married?"

He remembered how Kasey had asked the same thing. And then he wondered why she would, considering such a question usually was part of a come-on.

He studied the woman more closely and noted the skirt was a bit too tight, obviously to grab attention. She seemed to be hiding a kind of sadness. He noticed the wrinkles at the corners of her gray eyes and thought he might have underestimated her age. In any case, she was moving pretty quickly, whether she was a Petrucco spy or a lonely spinster on the make.

"Divorced," he answered reluctantly.

"Did you dump her or the other way around?"

He wanted to say this wasn't exactly the type of conversation two people who just met would have. But it was a bar. And even if she was a plain-Jane, there was something enticing about her.

"She dumped me."

"I'll bet that hurt."

He sighed and stared into the amber currents of his scotch.

"It did."

"She caught you messing around, didn't she."

It wasn't a question. Bruce tilted his glass and gnawed on some ice.

"We're all sinners," she said, realizing he wasn't going to respond and assuming she had been correct. "You should try to forget about her, because I can tell you're still hurting pretty bad."

He finished his drink and put the glass down on the bar.

"Yes, I am," he said quietly.

She put a hand on his forearm and squeezed.

"You want someone to help you get over her? At least for tonight?"

He crossed his brow. He was missing something here.

"What do you do?" he asked.

Her hand moved to his thigh.

"Oh, a little bit of everything. At least for a price."

"Jesus," he mumbled. A hooker.

Maybe it was the scotch or Tucker kicking his ass or his longing to be closer to Kasey or the fact that he was still stung by his broken marriage. Or maybe it was that this lady of the evening had hit the nail on the head: he was indeed lonely. But he felt compelled to ask.

"How much do you charge?"

"For you, five hundred for the night. Then whatever you want."

He thought about it and pulled out his wallet.

"Oh, I like a man who pays in advance," she said with a smile.

He fished out a twenty then gently pushed her hand off his leg.

"Linda, this is for keeping me company for a few minutes. Now if you don't mind, I'm going to move along. I'm kind of tired."

Her smile turned into a scowl as he got up and left another twenty for the bartender. The Lakers were stomping the Pistons anyway.

*

The next morning he stared into a cup of black coffee, unsure of what to do next. He thought about confronting Petrucco face-to-face. But he knew what he would be up against—layers of attorneys, bodyguards and personal valets protecting the guy. He didn't know if he could muster the energy to deal with that. He felt deep fatigue behind his eyes. He hadn't slept much because a part of him wished he had employed Linda's services.

Now he braced to tell Sam that he had nowhere to go with the abduction story, and that she might as well assign him to cover a circus.

"Hey." Bruce looked up to see a young man, one of the neophyte reporters who shared his newsroom, but whose name he didn't know.

"Yes?"

"Someone's up front to see you."

Bruce turned and looked over the ledge of his cubical to the front of the newsroom. His eyes widened. Officer Kasey Martin stood there clad in jeans and a

The East Side of Lauderdale

light-blue sports shirt, not the institutional green flight suit.

He jumped up and almost ran over to her, and he was about to give a warm hello. But upon closer inspection he saw that she was in a bad way. Her eyes were red, her hair was tussled, and her left cheek was bruised.

"Officer Martin, nice to see you," he said cautiously.

"Could we go somewhere private?" She was holding a folder.

"Yes, of course."

He led her to a conference room with an oval, dark, wooden desk.

"Can I get you some coffee?"

"Black," she said quietly, taking one of the many chairs.

He headed to the break room and filled a cup. Upon returning, he handed it to her and closed the conference room door. He took a seat two chairs away.

"That's good and hot," she said, after taking a sip, strands of dark hair falling around her face. "Thanks."

He considered asking why she looked like she been in a barroom brawl. But he already knew, and didn't want to risk embarrassing or inflaming her.

She took another sip then slid the folder toward him.

"Tucker's column was wrong," she said, her voice barely audible. "There aren't four missing women. As of this week, there are five."

*

Bruce opened the manila folder and saw the stack of missing persons' reports, including the name of Betty

Sue Curtis, which didn't immediately ring a bell. But then it did. She was the home shopping network host he had written about just a few days earlier.

The coincidence hit him and bothered him. On Monday, she was a smiling face in a feature. Three days later, she was an apparent victim. He wondered if there was a connection between his story and her disappearance. He was sure the police were curious about the same thing.

He leafed through the other reports and found Melinda Norman's name in the stack, as well as that of Mary Sims, Charlotte Baker and Janice Weslowski.

"So the fifth victim is Betty Sue?"

"Yes. By the way, the detectives are aware that you just wrote a story about her on Monday. Don't be surprised if one of them calls you on that."

Bruce nodded.

"Kasey, I don't know what to say."

"Tell the detectives the truth, that you were assigned to write about her—"

"I mean, I don't know what to say to you, to thank you for this information."

Kasey took a sip, eyes half shut, somehow resigned.

"No need to say anything."

"Can you fill me in on what happened to Betty Sue?"

"Mrs. Curtis was confirmed missing as of yesterday, when we found her car in a remote area on Southwest 128th Avenue. She was driving a silver E-Class Mercedes with a black convertible top. She was last seen on Wednesday, leaving work. Husband called us frantic that night."

The East Side of Lauderdale

"Was there any evidence of foul play?"

"Passenger-side window of the car was busted out. Her husband alerted us to the fact she kept a gun in the glove compartment and we found it near the car. It hadn't been fired, but it's still an indication things didn't go right for her."

Bruce pushed his chair back a bit and rubbed his chin.

"How could so many women end up missing and not make a splash?"

"What do you mean?"

"The press loves to spot trends and patterns. Here we have five respected businesswomen abducted in the past six months. It seems like there should have been an avalanche of coverage long before the Melinda Norman case."

Kasey shrugged.

"Obviously, the press didn't know about the other cases. For starters, these women were initially listed as missing-person cases, and missing persons don't get anybody excited. Fact is, it took the detectives quite awhile to put it together because the cases were so scattered."

Bruce sat back, still befuddled.

"Why did you bring this to me? Or are you also giving it to other media?"

"Just you."

"Then why just me?"

Kasey finished her coffee and put the paper cup down.

"I guess because you stood up for me with Jed. I felt like I owe you."

He cocked his head to one side.

"You're giving me this exclusive because you feel you owe me?"

"That's right."

Bruce took a moment to put together what he knew he needed to say.

"If that's the case, then I'm going to try to help you some more. Get away from him. I can see that he roughed you up again and it's obvious he's destroying your life. You should—"

"That's none of your business," she snapped, cutting him off.

"I just made it my business," he countered. "I like you, Kasey. I'm beholden to you, in fact, for all the information you've furnished. And I don't like sitting by while some ape beats on you. I can't figure out for the life of me why you would get involved with him in the first—"

But before he could go on, her face crunched up. She put her palms over her eyes and started to sob.

*

After a few awkward minutes, Bruce extended her his clean hanky. She took it without looking at him and wiped her eyes. She breathed in.

"After that whole thing at the bar, I tried to break it off with Jed a few nights ago," she said in a hoarse whisper. "He seemed like he was okay with it. We agreed to be friends. Then he shows up last night. Why I let him in … The son of a bitch was so damned rough."

The East Side of Lauderdale

He was hoping she would clarify that. Did she mean rough during sex? During an argument? Did he rape and beat her? In any case, why hadn't she filed criminal charges?

But she didn't expound, and he wasn't about to ask her to.

"You need to be aware of something," she said.

"What?"

"By giving you this information, I put you in danger."

"How?"

"I wanted you to have these files because I think you really want to help these women. But the thing is, I really wanted to hurt Jed, get him back. So first thing this morning, I went to the station, took the files from his desk, made copies and—"

"And if I run a story based on this information, the department will finger Jed as its leak," he said, finishing the thought for her.

"That's right. Which is why you need to be cautious if you write a story. He'll probably figure out that I set him up. No matter what, considering what happened the other night, he's already got reason to come looking for you. He'll want to know how you got the information."

"He hasn't come after me yet."

"He will. Trust me."

"I can take care of myself. I'm worried about you."

She got up, wiping her eyes with the back of her hand.

"I can take care of myself, too. Jeff, from here we're square, okay? I don't owe you. You don't owe me. Thanks for the coffee."

13.

"Hello, gentlemen!" Tucker sang as she approached the big round table at the Floridian restaurant, circled by the old men in their gray suits, regal ties and gold jewelry. But instead of their normal exuberance, they seemed subdued.

"What the hell is with you guys?"

Then she saw the stranger on the other side of the table. She took a seat between land baron Clayton McGreggor and illustrious barrister Bradley Crawford, making a point to kiss both on the cheek. Today Tucker was dressed in a lavender jacket, skirt and matching clogs. Even her nails and lipstick had a purple tinge.

"Hello dear," McGreggor said quietly.

"Sheryl, darling," Crawford said by way of greeting, equally subdued.

She snapped her fingers for coffee and gazed around table. She saw that County Commissioner Sidney Simon and restaurateur Kenton Cook looked down as they ate. She noted that State Attorney Harold Forest was absent.

She focused on the stranger. He had broad shoulders, ruddy cheeks and the rugged appearance of a dockworker. What was left of his black-dyed hair was greased straight back. He wore a gray flannel jacket and an open collar. In defiance to Florida statutes, a cigarette dangled from thin lips, which had some nearby patrons scowling in disgust.

Squinting through his smoke, he studied her back. He calmly stood and reached a big meaty hand over the table. She hesitantly put a soft hand in his and felt cold, hard muscle clamp down.

"Frank Petrucco," he said evenly.

Tucker snapped her hand back. This was the man she had identified as a prominent organized-crime figure, linked to the four missing women. She immediately wondered whether Petrucco had trailed her here, seeking retribution.

She looked to the other men. Normally, they were powerful captains of business. But now they seemed to be cowering, as if Petrucco had bullied his way to their table.

The reputed mobster was working on a plate of French toast between puffs. He grinned at Tucker as a waitress placed a mug of coffee in front of her. While Tucker gave the waitress a quick breakfast order, Petrucco calmly bent over and popped opened a black-leather briefcase that was resting at his feet. He pulled something out of it.

Then he slammed a newspaper down in the middle of the table. Glasses of orange juice and cups of coffee leaped. Tucker jumped, as did the others. The usually chaotic restaurant went quiet as patrons twirled around to see what was up.

The object of Petrucco's fury was a copy of the *Fort Lauderdale Post* with her accusatory column out front. Tucker half-expected a dead fish to roll out of it.

"I should let my dog squat on this," Petrucco said in a gravely voice.

Squaring her shoulders, Tucker met his angry stare.

"Listen," she said quietly, "I don't know what you intend here—"

"What I intend is to let you know this is a piece of garbage."

Tucker tried to keep her cool, taking a sip of coffee. But her hand quivered as her lips met the rim of the cup.

"I'm sorry if you disagree with my column, Mr. Petrucco. If you have a complaint, you should take it up with our paper's attorneys."

Petrucco laughed arrogantly, looking at the other men, hoping they would join him. But they squirmed uncomfortably.

Regaining himself, Frank Petrucco leaned toward her.

"Listen, sweetheart. I don't give a shit about your attorneys. I'm here for one reason."

Tucker expected him to produce a gun and leave her brains splattered on the floor. But she remained calm.

"What would that be?"

"To make sure you get it right next time."

With that, he produced another paper and slapped this one down, too.

"See this here? This paper got it right."

With a chubby index finger, he poked the *East Lauderdale Tattler,* specifically the story stripped across the top of that Monday morning's edition.

Tucker gingerly reached over and picked up the paper.

"May I?"

Petrucco nodded and took a puff.

Despite all eyes on her, she read intently. The story detailed five abductions, one more than she had reported. It went into depth on how the police now were convinced that one primary perpetrator likely was responsible and had accomplices working for him. And indeed, it made no mention of Petrucco.

She returned to the top of the story to check the by-line.

Jeff Bruce.

"Son of a bitch," she muttered.

"My name isn't even in that story," Frank Petrucco said, almost gloating. "And let me tell you something. I never had any kind of personal relationship with Mrs. Weslowski like you said in that piece of crap you wrote. The police fed you a line of bullshit and you bought it. I should sue your tight little ass for defamation of character."

She glared up at him, rolling up the *Tattler* in her hands.

"Why don't you do that, Mr. Petrucco. Meanwhile, my tight little ass is going do everything it can to see your big fat ass put away—for good."

She got up and departed just as the waitress delivered her order of toast and fruit. Her older gentleman friends sat, silent but distraught. Petrucco took a last drag on the nub of his cigarette and picked up his fork.

"Damn, I'm hungry," he said, stabbing his French toast.

*

She barely got to her car when she heard him call out to her.

"Sheryl. Please. Wait."

She turned to see Sidney Simon walking quickly after her, or at least as quickly as a man in his seventies could.

"Go away, Sidney."

She started to unlock the door to her Porsche, but the old county commissioner, wearing suspenders under his business suit, grabbed her arm.

"Please, this is important."

She whipped around.

"What, dammit?"

In his role as the County Commission chairman, Simon was known as a great orator, much like his father before him, a popular state senator. Both not only had the gift of gab, but also the ability to present clear, poignant arguments, making them influential politicians.

Simon's father, for instance, had used that gift to convince his fellow legislators to provide Henry Flagler with enough acreage to build a railroad from Jacksonville to Key West in the late 1800s. Thus, trainloads of visitors eventually flowed into Florida, boosting tourism to an enormous industry.

His son, Sidney, similarly, had used his persuasive powers to convince his fellow commissioners to build lots of condominium complexes in Broward County, in deference to his many developer friends, strangling the region with growth.

So, where the father had gone down in state history as an eloquent facilitator of the state's economic development, the son had earned a reputation as something of a sleazy fast-talker.

But for the moment, Simon, his bald dome gleaming in the morning sun, his gray hair and moustache making him look every bit his seventy-three years, stammered, struggling to find the right words.

"Sheryl, I ... I say this only because I love you like a daughter. You need to let go of this abduction business. I know it's a big story, but you should just drop it."

"You kidding me?"

"You pursue this and you'll get yourself in trouble, really big trouble. I'm telling you, it's not worth it."

Despite her agitated state, having been beaten by a second-rate newspaper and then belittled by a mobster, she laughed in the old man's face.

"Read my lips, Sidney. No way."

"I'm trying to warn you, Sheryl."

"Warn me about what? You think I'm afraid of Petrucco? Unlike you, I'm not going to let him push me around."

Simon looked down. His lips moved but no sound came out.

"Get out of my way, you doddering old goat."

She got in the car, and tires peeled as she backed out of the parking lot.

The East Side of Lauderdale

Simon shook his head and returned inside.

*

"Hey, you can't go in there!"

Tucker ignored the front desk secretary at the Broward State Attorney's Office, located in a top level of the County Courthouse complex. She stormed into Harold Forest's office and found him behind his giant work desk, feet kicked up leisurely over one end, leafing through some paperwork.

He gazed up at her with some surprise.

"Sheryl, I'm busy."

"And I'm in a snit. Where the hell were you this morning, Harry? You missed all the fun with this Frank Petrucco guy trying to intimidate me."

"He tried to intimidate you?"

"And failed. Where were you?"

"I was there, briefly. But the moment I saw him walk into the restaurant I walked out. I didn't want to have any kind of contact, considering he could easily be the target of prosecution by my office. What's the problem, Sheryl?"

She held the *East Lauderdale Tattler* in front of Forest's face.

"This is the problem, Harry, and the fact that some rat leaked this story to this miserable excuse for a newspaper. I got a feeling you know who it is."

"I have no idea what you're talking about."

She knocked his feet off his desk and sat down on the edge.

141

"The hell you don't. You know what I think, Harry? I think you *are* the rat. Why would you stab me in the back like that?"

Forest put his paperwork down and sighed.

"Listen, Sheryl, I didn't give that reporter anything. All I know is that somehow, he got a hold of some files that were atop a detective's desk."

"Which detective?"

"Peterson. Jed Peterson."

"So why in God's name is Peterson feeding this stuff to the *Tattler*?"

"I don't know that he is. If he is, he's in trouble."

Tucker hopped off the big desk.

"You know what, Harry? I thought we were friends. I guess I was wrong."

He got up in time to stop her at the door.

"Wait a minute, Sheryl. You know that if I could, I'd tell you everything. But we got a touchy situation here. Really touchy."

She continued walking into the hallway in an obvious huff.

Forest followed her, aware that members of his staff were watching. He spoke to her in hushed tones.

"Sheryl, dammit, you're taking advantage of a privileged relationship, and I thought we agreed we'd never do that, take advantage of each other."

She whipped around.

"Comes a time, Harry, when friends take advantage."

They stood facing each other for almost a full minute before Forest pointed her back into his office.

*

The East Side of Lauderdale

He laid it out as best he could, explaining that the police had been investigating Frank Petrucco long before he surfaced as a suspect in the abductions. And that was because Petrucco was a giant in the video-pornography business.

"He operates production studios here in Florida, the San Fernando Valley in California and Vegas," Forest said. "And he has an expansive distribution network."

Tucker pulled out her notebook.

"I knew about the porn operation from Detective Pena. He said there was nothing outwardly illegal about it, but that it might be a front for racketeering."

"Yes, but that's not what we're most interested in."

"What is?"

"You ever heard of rape videos? It's a whole genre of the industry. Most of them are staged. But the ones that sell for big bucks on the black market are very real. Real women, really abducted and really raped. We think Petrucco has made a number of these ghastly videos. And we think the local women who were abducted are quite possibly going to end up in some of them."

Tucker whistled. "Really."

"We've been keeping close tabs on the video market, but so far, none of the women have surfaced. If one does, we'll pounce on Petrucco hard."

"Jesus," Tucker muttered. "Incredible."

Forest raised his chin.

"Here's the touchy part. Turns out one of Petrucco's best customers is Sidney."

Tucker's jaw dropped.

"Sidney Simon? Our Sidney?"

"Our Sidney. However, to the best of our knowledge, he hasn't purchased any rape videos. Just mainstream stuff."

She thought about how Sidney had just asked her to let go of the abduction story. Now that request started to make sense.

"So you think Sidney is involved somehow?"

"Not necessarily. But his connection to Petrucco is a loose end. Even if he's not directly involved, Sidney may have knowledge of the abductions. That's why we have to play this situation very carefully. For now, he doesn't know that he's under surveillance."

Tucker got up and kissed Harold Forest on the cheek.

"Thanks, pal. You just made my day."

As she walked towards his door, Harold Forest jumped up.

"Sheryl, you're not going to write anything about Sidney, right?"

She just smiled and kept going.

14.

"What the hell happened?"

Samantha Pauline VanDermark held her forehead in her palms as she stared down at the *Fort Lauderdale Post*, spread out on her desk. Bruce sat in the hot seat in front of her. The door to her office was closed.

"I got beat," he quietly conceded. "Again."

She shook her head. Although she was given to theatrics, Bruce sensed this scene was for real. She was legitimately upset.

"Crushed is more like it. I was so proud of you yesterday, Jeff. Your story on the five abductions put us way out in front. But this—" she slapped an open palm on Sheryl Tucker's column, "this makes us look bad. *Really* bad."

"Sam—"

"Tucker finds out that the women probably were abducted for rape videos. On top of that, she reveals that Commissioner Simon is a porn addict and could be linked to all this. How did we miss these things, Jeff? How did we miss such huge developments?"

Bruce was tired of punishing himself and getting upset when Tucker bested him. So his voice rose a little louder than he intended.

"I'll tell you how, Sam. The police are playing favorites. And Sheryl Tucker happens to be their favorite. That's one of the nice perks when you work for large metropolitan newspaper. I don't think she would have been nearly as insightful if she worked for a small, society newsletter like—"

He caught himself, knowing to insult the low profile of the *East Lauderdale Tattler* was a direct affront to Sam, who, again, had been gracious enough to give him a second chance when few others would.

Sitting up, brow furrowing, she picked up on the barb.

"Is that supposed to be an excuse? Jeff, you've got to do better than blame your employer for your own ineptitude. You just didn't dig deep enough."

"I did my best, Sam."

"I don't think so."

Both sat silent for a long moment, avoiding eye contact.

Sam finally spoke in a controlled tone.

"Listen carefully, Jeff. You need to come out ahead and stay ahead. We both know that, with your past experience as an investigative reporter, you have the ability to do so. But if this happens again—"

"You'll fire me."

"Yes. That's right. Jeff, I know you think I'm young and wet behind the ears. And I admit that I was wrong for not putting much stock in this story at first. But now I know the stakes are high. And you need to realize

The East Side of Lauderdale

that, too. Society newsletter or not, we need to take ownership of the story because it directly affects the heart of our readership."

Bruce sensed desperation in her warning. He guessed that the publisher, that fine old gentleman and former mayor, Joe Petruska, had called Sam onto the carpet probably that very morning. It was entirely possibly that her job was on the line, too.

He nodded.

"I'll step it up, Sam. And I'm sorry about the society newsletter crack."

Expressionless, she pointed at her door for him to go.

*

Bruce sauntered into the break room, seeking a place to escape. He knew the young reporters in the newsroom had witnessed the closed-door meeting and were talking about how Tucker had murdered him again and how his job was on the line. There weren't many secrets around a small shop like the *East Lauderdale Tattler*.

He was suddenly saddened that he didn't have a single friend out there, not one person he could talk to or confide in. None of the reporters wanted anything to do with him simply because he didn't fit in. He wondered if any of them knew anything about his background, that he had been let go from his previous job.

He grabbed a cup of coffee, took a deep breath and returned to his desk, sensing his coworkers staring at him. Sitting down, he surveyed the accumulated paperwork spread over his work area, wondering where to start. He gazed at that morning's copy of the *Post*, lying on his desk. Tucker's haughty mug stared right through him. At least for this day she would serve as a reminder that maybe Sam was right; maybe he hadn't dug hard enough.

Mustering some mental energy, he was about to pick up the phone and call the public information officer at the Police Department. But the phone rang first, and amazingly, it was Detective Carlos Pena.

"Detective, what a pleasant—"

"Cut the small talk, Mr. Bruce. I need to know: How did you get the idea to do the story on Betty Sue Curtis?"

"Why do you ask?"

"You know damn well why. Mrs. Curtis disappeared only three days after your story about her came out. So do me a big favor and stop fucking with me."

Bruce wasn't surprised by the sudden harshness. He had dealt with a lot of cops in his career and knew all about their intimidation tactics.

"Am I a suspect, detective?"

"If you were a suspect, we'd be having this conversation here at the station. I'm trying to tie up loose ends and the coincidence is bothersome."

"My editor assigned it to me."

"Your editor have any kind of personal relationship with Mrs. Curtis?"

"You should ask my editor that question."

"I intend to do that, Mr. Bruce, but for now I'm asking you," Pena barked.

Bruce sighed. "Not that I know of."

The East Side of Lauderdale

After a cold silence filled by Bruce drumming his fingers on his desk, Pena continued, "When you interviewed Mrs. Curtis, did she hint that anything unusual was going on in her life?"

"No, she didn't."

"Is there any light at all you can shed on this? Why this woman appears in your story then disappears?"

"Not really."

"Then thanks for all your help."

Bruce spoke up before Pena hung up.

"Wait. Detective, while I have you on the phone, I was wondering if you saw Sheryl Tucker's column today and whether you could confirm—"

"I have nothing to say about that column."

"But I just wanted to know if—"

"Have to run. Again, thanks for nothing."

Bruce distinctly heard Pena mutter the word, "asshole," before slamming the phone down. He couldn't help but smile, knowing he had gotten under the detective's skin. But then he sat back and resumed looking at Tucker's mug. She had clobbered him yet again, and he wasn't sure that he could dig himself out of the hole that she had put him in.

*

Three hours later, Bruce was no further along than when he started. Seeking some kind of police comment, he had called the Police Chief's office and was told under no circumstance would the Department confirm or deny the information in Tucker's column. Sidney Simon was unreachable. And someone claiming to be Frank Petrucco's front man gave him a flat, "no comment."

Bruce decided this was a good time to have lunch. Dodging heavy traffic, he walked across Federal Highway to a chain-operated sub shop and ordered an Italian with everything on it, chips, and a large Diet Coke. He was happy that at this hour, almost two o'clock, the place was empty. He took a seat by a window, where he could watch the world go by.

He took a huge first bite, pickle juice and mayonnaise trickling down his chin. As he chewed, he realized that he had intentionally avoided calling Officer Kasey Martin, even though she had been his best source on the abduction story. But then, she had made it clear that she never wanted to talk to him again.

He took yet another big bite, and as he did so, the front door of the sub shop swung open. A lovely woman with the comportment of a movie star breezed in. Without hesitation, she came to his table and sat down across from him.

For a moment he actually thought it was Angelina Jolie.

Then he realized who it was, and it was equally surprising.

She put down an elbow and rested her chin in an open palm.

"Know who I am?"

"Shermph Tucmpher," he said with mouth full.

Tucker smiled, revealing a chorus of perfect white teeth. She was wearing a red skirt and a sleeveless white blouse. A gold chain with a crucifix rested at the base

The East Side of Lauderdale

of her neck, and her arms had distinct muscular tone. Her hair was pinned back on either side of her head.

"That's right. And now I know who you are."

"Whof wouf thaf bef?"

"You're the guy who got fired for plagiarism."

Bruce dabbed his mouth with a napkin and tried to hide his surprise. Seeing his attempt to be nonchalant, Tucker grinned.

"About two months ago, I read this story in the *American Journalism Review*," she said. "It was about this hotshot reporter at the *Dallas Register* taking a tremendous fall. You have to keep in mind that the *Register* is one of the most respected newspapers in the country, and you pretty much have to be a star to get on their staff—just as you would at the *New York Times* or the *Washington Post*."

Bruce took a sip of soda and cleared his palate.

"That so?"

"Yes, that's so. Anyway, this particular reporter, who had already won a ton of awards, launches into this major investigation and finds this fundamentalist extremist group had established sleeper terrorist cells throughout the Southwest, Arizona, Texas and New Mexico. Only the feds don't know this until they read about it in the *Register*. As turns out, he makes the FBI look like a bunch of monkeys for missing this huge terrorist threat. But then the feds move in and likely prevent another Nine-Eleven-like scenario. All of the sudden, this reporter is on a beeline for a Pulitzer. And then you know what happened?"

"Tell me. I'm intrigued."

"He rips off a twenty-paragraph segment of a *New York Times* story. A story that detailed how the al Qaeda terrorists are patient, willing to wait decades before springing an attack. He copied it, word-for-word. When his editors discovered this, the reporter was unceremoniously fired and his name was quickly withdrawn from Pulitzer contention. The guy was subsequently banished from working at any credible newspaper and ends up working for a two-bit rag here in Fort Lauderdale. Any of this sound familiar?"

"Vaguely."

She sat back and demurely crossed her legs.

"So the question is, what happened, Jeff? Why'd you do it?"

Bruce shrugged.

"Just one of those things, I guess."

She ignored his smugness.

"Considering your level of experience, you didn't need to copy a single word of that *Times* story. You could have easily gotten the information on your own. So, obviously, you came apart at the seams when the pressure was on. Does that pretty much sum up the situation?"

Bruce took another sip. He picked up a potato chip and nibbled on it, declining to comment. She exhaled heavily, not out of vexation, but more out of sensing her mission had been accomplished.

"Anyway, Jeff, I dropped by because I wanted you to know: I know who you are. You're a guy who had a shot at stardom but took a sad, pathetic plunge. My guess is, because you couldn't take the heat while working the big story."

The East Side of Lauderdale

She waited for Bruce's retort, but all he did was wrinkle his nose.

Tucker smiled coyly. "And here you are, in over your head again."

She got up and left, just as breezily as she came in, leaving him speechless, her words stinging more than she could know.

15.

The truth was, Bruce had become a distraction. So Tucker had waited in her car in the *Tattler's* parking lot until she saw him come out of his building. She almost accosted him right there, but instead watched him walk across the street to the sub shop. She drove to small eatery, followed him in and did her best to discourage him from pursuing the abduction story any further. She had a hunch she had been successful, evidenced by the pathos in his eyes.

Now she returned to her office in mid-afternoon, determined to focus on Sidney Simon. Her column that morning had revealed his lust for pornography and his connection to Frank Petrucco, but she wanted him on record to explain what he was thinking, his motivations. In other words, another hatchet job ripping into the County Commission chairman was in order.

She took no joy in going after Simon. Until this Petrucco business surfaced, she had considered the old man a dear friend, no matter his unctuous political image. But Simon was a prominent government official

The East Side of Lauderdale

who now had mud on his shoes, and she was a bulldog journalist with an obligation to force him to come clean.

The problem was Simon had vanished. She couldn't reach him at his commission office or home. And no one at the Broward Government Center knew where he was. Tucker guessed he had gone into seclusion, too embarrassed to face public ridicule. But there was another, more disturbing possibility—that Petrucco had disposed of Simon to prevent him from spilling damaging information to the cops.

As she pondered these things, her phone rang.

"Sheryl, I'm shocked and dismayed over this morning's column. How could you lay into Sidney like that?"

It was Kenton Cook, the rotund and normally jovial restaurateur, who obviously hadn't called to schmooze.

"You seem a bit upset, Kenton."

"Don't be snide, Sheryl. That was a lousy thing to do, revealing that Sidney buys pornography, like it's some big crime. Hell, I buy porn, your mailman buys porn, and your father probably buys porn."

"My father's been dead for almost twenty years, Kenton."

"Well, my sincerest apologies, but you get my point. People buy pornography these days like they do bath soap. It's no big deal. Besides that, Sidney always been on your side and considers you a friend. After all the lovely mornings we've spent together, how could you betray him like that?"

Tucker sat up, resenting his biting tone.

"Friends or not, I had no choice, Kenton. Sidney is under investigation because he didn't just buy pornography—he bought it in large quantity from a person linked to the abductions. And that's why the police think Sidney might know something about the women."

"That's ridiculous. Sidney knows absolutely nothing about the disappearance of—"

"And you know this, how?" she asked sharply.

The plump and bald Kenton Cook went silent, except for heavy breathing.

"Let me ask you something, Kenton. Do you know where Sidney is? Have you talked to him today?"

She could hear Cook lick his lips.

"I have no idea where he is. I spoke to Sidney yesterday, and he told me how he tried to warn you to stay clear of that story, that there could be trouble. After today's column, he's probably going to have to resign in disgrace."

Tucker furrowed her brow, sensing something way out of whack.

"Why all the attitude, Kenton? You get pissed at me because I'm doing my job? What the hell's going on?"

Cook took a deep breath, the air whistling through his nostrils.

"I'll tell you what's going on, Sheryl. It so happens that Mr. Petrucco is a friend. He is a loyal and frequent visitor to my restaurants. And it might surprise you to know that he does legitimate business with some of the others in our breakfast group. For instance, I think he's worked out a land deal here and there with Clayton.

The East Side of Lauderdale

That's why he was welcomed to our table yesterday morning."

Now Tucker was quiet, not quite believing what she was hearing. Her entire breakfast club had an association with the main suspect in the abductions? While all along she had assumed they were as clean as snowflakes?

"That's interesting," she muttered.

"Yes, well, that in mind, Mr. Petrucco called me this afternoon. Because he knows that I'm close to you, he asked me to relay a request."

"Which is what?"

"He wants a retraction for your saying that he had a role in those women being abducted. And I must agree that a retraction would be in order. You made him look guilty as sin with no basis in fact."

An icy tingling shot down Tucker's spine. Now Cook was leaving open another amazing possibility—that he, like Sidney Simon, was implicated in this nasty business. For that matter, maybe all her old buddies were.

"You think a retraction would be in order," she repeated slowly.

"I most certainly do."

"And if I don't do this retraction?"

Cook took another moment.

"It was like Sidney told you. You could be in big trouble."

Tucker didn't like real or implied threats, and her first reaction was to boil over. But she saw an opportunity here.

"Kenton, if I'm going to do a retraction, I need to talk to Petrucco face-to-face. He needs to tell me exactly what I wrote that was wrong. Will you call Mr. Petrucco on my behalf and tell him I need to talk to him personally?"

She heard more labored breathing on the other end of the line.

"I'll call you back."

He did so ten minutes later.

"Mr. Petrucco asked that you meet him in the grand ballroom of the Pier 66 at seven o'clock, tonight. He'll be attending a fundraiser there. For the opera."

Tucker didn't say thank you for setting up the meeting or goodbye. She just hung up, sad that she thought she knew Kenton Cook, but really didn't.

*

Pier 66 was one of Fort Lauderdale's most popular luxury hotels, standing tall on the north edge of Port Everglades. It was a tubular structure with a lounge atop that slowly rotated 360 degrees, providing a spectacular view of South Florida's waterways, marinas, golf courses, condos and business districts.

Shortly after seven that evening, Tucker found the grand ballroom, where the lights were already dimmed. The place was shoulder to shoulder with tuxedoes and long evening gowns. Waiters served chutes of champagne and fancy hors d'oeuvres. Dozens of large, round tables were adorned with flower centerpieces. A seven-piece band played mellow background music on a stage.

Knowing she needed to fit in, Tucker wore a strapless, midnight-blue gown that hid all but the

The East Side of Lauderdale

pointy toes of her white high heels. She also donned a diamond necklace and carried a small, white purse.

It took a while, but she found Petrucco seated at a table with seven other guests. He was sipping bourbon neat, smiling, and making small talk with a young blonde, her hair frilled up in a beehive. She looked dazzling in a white-sequin evening gown. The large rock on her finger indicated she was the trophy wife. He also was smoking, even though that was strictly prohibited at a fete like this.

Tucker took a chair next to him, but on the opposite side of the blonde, who broke into a cold stare. Petrucco didn't immediately see Tucker because he was facing the other way.

"So you want me to run a retraction?"

He turned slowly to glance at her, the smile fading. He turned back to his sexy, young wife, leaned over, and whispered something in her ear. She nodded and got up, apparently dispatched to get a fresh drink, glaring at Tucker as she went. Petrucco swiveled on his seat to meet Tucker head-on.

She grinned at this.

"Well, do you?" she asked again. "Want a retraction?"

His face was a craggy, granite scowl.

"First you write a column that accuses me of being the one responsible for abducting all these women. Then you say I videotaped them being raped. And now you come in here and act like you want to pee in my face. Yeah. I want a retraction. And a little respect wouldn't hurt, either."

Tucker shrugged.

"First of all, I didn't say any of those things. The police did. And they didn't come right out and say you actually did those things. They called you a person of interest. So you tell me exactly what I wrote that was wrong. Maybe I'll consider it. The retraction that is. Respect, that's a whole other deal."

Squinting through his cigarette smoke, Petrucco leaned toward her.

"You got a smart mouth on you, you know that? It's not so much that you got something wrong as the way you put it. It *implies* I did something wrong."

A server came over with a silver tray full of champagne glasses. Tucker plucked one off and took a sip.

"Let me ask you directly, Mr. Petrucco. Did you have anything to do with the abductions of those women?"

Petrucco let out a smoker's coarse laugh.

"I most certainly did not."

"And those women will never be featured in your rape videos?"

His face turned red, and a vein popped out of his left temple.

"No, they never will be. Those videos are all scripted and performed by professional actors, and I can prove that."

"Yet, while they won't say it publicly, the police consider you the prime suspect. How do you explain that, Mr. Petrucco?"

A man who liked to get in people's faces, he leaned so close this time that she could smell the pungent combination of smoke and whisky on his breath.

The East Side of Lauderdale

"I explain it like this," he said through gritted teeth. "Either run a retraction saying you don't know from horseshit about my involvement in this thing or someone's going to adjust your snotty little attitude."

Her mouth dropped open, astonished at how boorish he was.

"I don't like threats, Mr. Petrucco."

He took a deep drag from his cigarette and smiled.

She looked around at the other people at the table, including three middle-aged women with faces caked with makeup, sitting with their obedient husbands. They were chatting merrily, completely unaware of the growing tensions nearby. Tucker picked up a fork and rapped her champagne class, loud enough that even people at a few surrounding tables looked up.

"Anyone hear this man make a death threat against me?" Tucker asked rather loudly. "Anyone here got the guts to be a witness for me in court?"

The guests wore blank faces, none daring to respond. Tucker turned back to the reputed mobster.

"No matter, Mr. Petrucco. Under subpoena, at least one or two of these fine people will testify you just threatened my life. Now do you want to retract that threat, Mr. Petrucco?"

It was an obvious mockery of his request to retract the allegations in her column.

"Chrissake," he spat. "You don't know who you're dealing with here."

"And apparently you don't realize who you're dealing with."

Oddly, in that strained moment, she took careful notice of her surroundings and saw the face. She furrowed her brow. Clayton McGreggor sat a few tables away. He made quick eye-contact then looked away. She wanted to gaze around to see if any other breakfast buddies were here; Kenton Cook, Bradley Crawford, Harold Forest or maybe even Sidney Simon.

But Frank Petrucco demanded all her attention.

He inhaled deeply on his cigarette and exhaled a blue plume of smoke.

"Somehow we got off on the wrong foot, you and me. Let me take a crack at this from another angle. I'm asking nice: Will you please write a follow-up story, noting that the police don't have anything solid to suggest I'm involved with those women? And while you're at it, throw in that Sidney bought those videos to give away as presents for his friends."

She laughed, though it was forced.

"Not a chance."

"Chrissake," he spat again. "You should—"

Before he could continue, a photographer approached the table—a freelancer hired to document all the merriment at the lavish affair.

"Can I get you all to smile?" he said in a polite, rushed tone.

Petrucco suddenly leaned over and put an arm around Tucker. His grip on her shoulder was as powerful as a reptilian jaw.

"What are you doing?" she protested.

"Look at the birdie," he said, smiling into the camera.

The flash went off, capturing a bewildered look on Tucker and a gleam in Petrucco's eye. The photographer,

The East Side of Lauderdale

as it turned out, would later submit this photo to the *East Lauderdale Tattler*.

Petrucco let go of her and took another long drag. She rubbed her shoulder where he had grabbed her. Now he spoke in a confidential tone.

"Sweetheart, let me tell you how I really do business. I ask someone for a favor and that favor either gets done, or someone gets hurt. So you can put on a big show and get your panties all in a wad. But I'm sure you'll do the right thing and run that retraction. And after that, who knows? Maybe you and me can get to be really close friends. Know what I mean?"

With that he placed a big, meaty hand on her knee.

"You son of a bitch," she hissed, pushing his hand away.

She heaved what was left of her champagne in his face, got up, and stormed away. Petrucco took the splash with little reaction. He pulled out a hanky and wiped off his face. Then he waved a hand, like it was all nonsense.

"Let's get back to the party, folks. Show's over."

The people at his table and those nearby took only momentary notice of the incident, then politely returned to their conversations, drinks, and dancing. What nobody saw was Frank Petrucco's big meaty hands clench into fists.

*

Tucker charged straight to the *Post* newsroom, yelling at Richard Bloom as she reached her office.

"My column for tomorrow will be on Frank Petrucco threatening to kill me unless I retract today's column."

Then she slammed her door, knowing that, once again, the entire newsroom operation would have to retool to accommodate another major story.

Bloom, who had been seated at his desk, playing solitaire, winced.

"That's nice," he said only to himself.

16.

Night was falling as the jetliner appeared on the western horizon, its silhouette descending through fading, crimson hues. Sitting in his car, not far from the runway, Bruce watched it land, smoke belching from its wheels.

Then he returned his attention to the 737 parked thirty yards in front of him at the Royal International hangar, on the north side of Fort Lauderdale-Hollywood International Airport. His VW was in the company's parking lot, up against a perimeter fence around the aircraft ramp. A McDonald's bag containing two cheeseburgers and fries sat on the seat next to him, nourishment for a stakeout.

He had been keeping an eye on the Royal International compound, specifically the 737, for a few nights now. Although interested in two other private jets that took off in the same hour on the night Melinda Norman disappeared, he was convinced the twin-engine Boeing in front of him had been the one that whisked her away.

For starters, he thought it odd that such a big plane had no logo or company name painted on its white and blue fuselage—only a tail number. By running that number through a federal aviation database, he determined that a firm called RTE, Inc. owned it. By tracing RTE through a Secretary of State database, he discovered it was a ghost corporation with only a post office box for an address. That's when he knew something wasn't right. How often does an anonymous entity operate a $50 million jet?

But other than overhearing the conversation of the two men, so far he had seen nothing suspicious. And it looked like that would be the case on this evening. The 737 was dark and quiet.

Out of boredom more than hunger, he pulled a cheeseburger from the bag. He took a bite and fiddled with his radio until he found a Miami Heat game.

Then he heard the footsteps coming from behind the car. He whipped around to look through the rear window. No one was there, but he sensed a presence. He put his right hand on the ignition key, ready to start up and bolt.

A beam of a bright light hit him in the face, coming from the passenger side window. He put his left hand to his brow and saw someone holding a flashlight. He hoped it was a security guard.

The dark, tall figure leaned down and looked in.

"Whatcha doing in there, sir?"

Bruce squinted, trying to get the person's face to come into focus.

"Just watching airplanes," he said cautiously.

"Would you like some company?"

The East Side of Lauderdale

"Jesus," Bruce muttered, recognizing the voice, relaxing his hands. "What are you—"

"Just happened to be in the neighborhood."

Officer Kasey Martin, wearing her drab-green flight suit, opened the door and hopped in. Bruce picked up the McDonald's bag just before she smashed down on it. She rested her big, police-issue flashlight on the floor at her feet then snatched the food bag out of his hand.

"I'm starving. Hope you don't mind."

She pulled out the second cheeseburger and ripped it from its wrapper.

"No problem," he said. "There are some fries in there, too."

"God, thanks," she said, stuffing half the burger in her mouth. She also managed to get a few fries in, as well.

"How did you know where to—" But then he remembered how he had told her about his private stakeouts, and she just gazed at him until she chewed enough to swallow.

"Detective Bruce," she said with a giggle, then took another big bite.

"I thought I had ... seen the last of you after you came to my office," he said, unable to take his eyes off of her.

She had to chew and swallow again before answering.

"Yeah, well, I was having a bad day. Can I have your Coke?"

He passed the big drink over to her and she drank from his straw without hesitation, which he found to be strangely erotic.

She turned and caught him staring.

Ken Kaye

"What? You don't think I'm lady-like?"

He raised his eyebrows.

"I think you're very lady-like. I was wondering if I might ask you something kind of personal."

"Shoot."

"Where are you from? I mean originally."

She sipped some more and pondered the question.

"Where do you think I'm from?"

He wanted to say China, or maybe the Philippines. Instead, he ventured, "Indonesia?"

She burst out laughing, putting a hand to her mouth.

"Indonesia! Where the hell is that?"

"Somewhere way out there," he mumbled, feeling stupid.

"My parents are from the Dominican Republic. I'm a Latina. And if you're wondering where my *I want-to-be-in-Amereeeca* accent is, I was born and raised in North Miami Beach. But I do speak a little *espanol*."

"*Yo tambien, pero yo hablo mal el espanol*," he said, attempting to say he spoke the language, too, only poorly.

"*Por el contrario, lo habla muy bien*!"

"What did you say?"

"Never mind."

"Anyway, Martin isn't exactly a Hispanic name."

"It's my stepfather's name. My mother remarried. Her maiden name was Zorilla and my real father's name is Rodriguez. So my full proper name used to be Maria Dinorah Zorilla Rodriguez. Then my stepdad nicknamed me Kasey, I guess because it's more American."

The East Side of Lauderdale

"Jesus. I was only off by about four continents."

She giggled and took the last bite of her cheeseburger. She looked at what was left of his cheeseburger, which he had been holding. She didn't even have to ask, he just gave it to her.

"Thanks," she said, eating the remains in one gulp. "I was really hungry."

"Never would have guessed," he muttered.

She patted her mouth with a napkin.

"I ran a DMV check on the license plate numbers you gave me on the two guys who were talking dirty. Care to hear what I found?"

He nodded, pleasantly surprised that she had followed through.

"Yes, I would."

She pulled a small notebook from the top zipper pocket of her flight suit and flipped to the first page.

"The van is registered to one Brad Holman, who has a Fort Lauderdale address on Seventeenth Street. The pickup was registered to a Ray Morgan, who also lives Fort Lauderdale on Fourth Street. I did a background check, including running them through the FBI's criminal database, and found both are licensed airline pilots with no prior offenses of any sort. So your dirty talkers are apparently squeaky clean."

Bruce was still troubled.

"Guess I was off-base with them. But I'm still convinced that jet had something to do with the women disappearing. Would it be possible to search it? The police could get a warrant. There might be evidence one or more of the women were on board. Hair, fibers, that kind of stuff."

She put away the notebook and swallowed the last of his Coke.

"No way, Jeff."

"Why not?"

"Because a plane search is no different from a car search or a house search. To execute a warrant you need reasonable cause which, unfortunately, we don't have."

Bruce looked over at the big plane and sighed.

"I guess that leaves me back at square one."

Both were quiet as cool night air settled in.

Then she turned to him.

"Not to change the subject, but why did you screw up?"

*

Even in dim light, she could see that he was caught off-guard. He immediately started fidgeting with his hands.

"What do you mean?"

"If you don't want to tell me, that's all right. I don't like to talk about my past either."

He chuckled nervously.

"I really don't know what—"

"You were once one of the top reporters in the country. I saw where you wrote this one fabulous story about Air Force One, all the adventures the various presidents had on board. You won some big award for it, didn't you?"

He hesitantly nodded, remembering the story well. It was one of the many he devoted himself to, keeping him in the newsroom up to sixteen hours a day and

The East Side of Lauderdale

away from home. He continued working his hands nervously, wondering just how extensively she had probed into his past.

"And there were lots of other stories like that, from the Mad Cow scare out West to how Neo-Nazis were trying to take over Idaho. Now you work for a tiny paper, writing ditzy features about me and my dumb night-flights. Jeff, as you can see, it wasn't hard to find out all about you. There's quite a bit right on the Internet."

He looked down, obviously flustered.

"Why would you even think to run a check on me?"

"I wanted to make sure the one person I have been feeding information doesn't have a rap sheet, that's why."

"Do I?"

"No. But on the other hand you were fired from the Dallas Register for plagiarism. That sounds pretty serious."

He stared at her for a long moment, thinking of the coincidence that Tucker had revealed she, too, had unearthed his horrible secret. He realized Kasey was waiting for an explanation.

"I'll give you the short version," he said quietly. "It all started and ended with Beth. We met in college and married young. She became a bank manager, I became an obsessed journalist."

He breathed in.

"I think we honestly loved each other, at least at one time. But our marriage was never really on solid footing. She wanted a family, kids, the minivan. She wanted to get pregnant in the worst way, but it just didn't happen. I guess because I wasn't home all that much. I was always out on assignment, and when I did get home—"

"You were too tired to pay your wife any attention," Kasey injected.

"Something like that. To cut to the chase, after a while, we did nothing but fight. No matter what I did, it was wrong. She'd jump on me if I bought the wrong brand of milk at the grocery store. I began to spend more and more time at work, and the truth is I just didn't want to go home. But then one day, I did. Early. And there they were. In our bed. In the middle of the afternoon. Two corporate suits were placed neatly over the chair. Hers and his."

"Oh my gosh."

Bruce grimaced.

"Yeah. He turned out to be another manager at her bank. They actually had been having these afternoon trysts for months. After I walked in on them that day, she just sat up and said, 'it's not my fault,' then told me to get out."

"Ow."

"My life pretty much turned upside down from there. We were divorced within two months. And on the day the divorce was final, I went into the newsroom, picked up that *New York Times* story and just started typing. I knew it was blatant plagiarism. But truth is I don't know why I did it, exactly. I saw this shrink who told me it was misplaced anger. But as I look back on it now, I think it was more about being lost than being angry."

The East Side of Lauderdale

He stopped to let it all sink in. Kasey turned away from him to study the big jet parked out on the ramp, its hulk silent and lonely.

"That's a sad story," she finally said. "You want my take?"

"I guess so."

"From the sound of it, your wife wasn't messing around because she was loose or evil. She did it because you weren't there for her. So maybe you didn't love her as much as you think you did. Maybe you were so engrossed in yourself that you didn't care that much about her. Maybe you got what you deserved."

His brow crinkled up in confusion.

"I was engrossed in my work—not myself—because I wanted to make a difference," he said, perhaps too defensively.

She turned back to him, meeting his wide-eyed stare.

"Jeff, I didn't say that to hurt you. But I know how your wife felt. My whole life I've been hooking up with men who put me second, and the truth is, I'm tired of it."

He tried to read her face, her emotions. But now she was looking away again, seemingly thinking about her own past emotional calamities.

"Why did you come here tonight?" he asked.

"I wanted to fill you in on the license plate information."

"That's the real reason?"

She pursed her lips.

"No. The real reason is because I've been thinking about you. I was thinking how you were pretending to be a cop. How you turned what little information I gave you into some pretty good stories. How you really want to find and help those poor women. How you risked your life for me, standing up to Jed. So, you got me interested. But, Jeff, you just revealed something … "

"I was just being honest."

"I appreciate that. But by your own admission, you're a man who doesn't have time for anyone but himself. You should ask yourself why that is, Jeff. Maybe deep down you're trying too hard to be a winner, or at least avoid being a loser."

She grabbed her flashlight from the floor, popped the door handle and stepped out of his car.

"Thanks for the burger."

Then she was gone yet again, leaving Bruce in growing darkness.

17.

He spent much of the night hunched over the counter of a Waffle House on Federal Highway, gazing at nothing. A cup of cold coffee kept him company, while a middle-aged waitress sat behind the cash register, reading the Bible, and an old man, likely homeless, camped out in a corner booth, muttering.

Physically exhausted and emotionally spent, Bruce thought how sadly remarkable it was that two women had sought him out to let him know how pathetic he was. Kasey had implied he was a loser for putting work before his wife. Tucker had inferred he was a milksop who cracked in the face of pressure.

Their message hit hard.

In the middle of this lonely, November night, he realized it was time to move on. He would return to the *Tattler*, clean out his desk, leave Sam a terse resignation letter and be gone before first light. The Rockies seemed appealing. He would settle somewhere like Aspen and do something like deliver pizza for a while. Eventually, he would sort out his life and plan a new future.

Ken Kaye

Maybe that would involve government work or teaching creative writing at a university. But he was through with journalism, tired of its frustrations. At four in the morning, he left ten dollars on the counter and walked out. The waitress never looked up from her Bible and the old man kept muttering.

Bruce drove toward his office as the night grew darker yet.

When he arrived at the *Tattler*, he parked by the front door and never did see the motorcycle glide in behind him, its engine and front light off.

*

He swiped his security pass in an electronic reader, and the front door released its lock. As he pushed the door open, someone slapped the back of his head with an open palm—hard.

He stumbled forward and fell, sliding on his hands and knees across the carpeted newsroom foyer. Aghast, he rolled over to see who had attacked him. There, under subdued security lights, stood Detective Jed Peterson, snorting and angry.

"Hiya, pal. Remember me?"

The mountain of a man leaned down, grabbed Bruce by the shirt collar, hoisted him to back his feet, and slapped him again with the force of a bat cracking against a baseball. The flash of pain rendered Bruce almost immediately defenseless.

Peterson's eyes were wild, and his face flushed red.

"You thought I'd forget about you? What you did to me?"

The East Side of Lauderdale

Peterson administered another ringing slap, this one a backhand. Bruce's head snapped left, his eyes went hazy, and his arms slack.

"Listen, I'll give you this; you sure blindsided me but good over at the bar. But you think I wasn't coming after you?"

Bruce put up a weak forearm, hoping to block the next slap. But Peterson read it and backhanded him again. Bruce's head snapped left again and he was on the verge of blacking out. Only Peterson's grasp on his collar kept him from collapsing.

"But you know what your biggest mistake was? You went and spent more time with my girl—after I warned you to stay clear."

With what little mental fortitude he had left, Bruce managed to grin and slur, "She hates you, Jed."

The big man pulled him in tighter.

"Wha'd you say?"

"Kasey. She hates you. You might think in some demented way that she actually loves you. But trust me. She hates you. The only reason she ever went out with you was to punish herself. You know, for that deal she was involved in where the guy killed an officer and his mother, then himself."

"You don't know what in the hell you're talking about."

"Yes, I do. And so do you. But now she's tired of being hounded, and at this point, she'd be justified in pulling a gun on you, Jed, blowing your head off. In fact, I'd be happy to testify on her behalf how you've stalked her, abused her."

Ken Kaye

"You little pansy, you'll never get the chance to testify."

Bruce smiled sardonically, knowing what was coming.

"Go ahead, ya big ape. Do your best."

In the dim light, Peterson's face contorted into pure rage.

"Wha'd you call me?"

"A big, stinking ape."

A growl came up from the bottom of Peterson's throat as he clenched a fist. He pulled back his right arm to slug Bruce in the face.

But suddenly, an object smashed down on the back of Peterson's head. The sound was akin to a hammer squishing into a cantaloupe. The big man's body went limp and he fell to the floor, releasing his grip on Bruce. Blood trickled from the back of his head.

Bruce looked up to see Sam, his editor, standing there with a five iron. Her hips were swiveled around as though she had teed off and was admiring the arc of the ball.

Wobbly and disoriented, Bruce gawked at her in amazement. He tried to ask how she had managed to rescue him. But all he could do was stare and stammer. And then he noticed: She was wearing only a bra and panties.

"Always knew this thing would come in handy," she said, breathing hard, referring to the golf club she kept in the corner of her office.

"Why are you here?" Bruce finally asked, still slurring his words, but now leaning on a nearby desk to keep his balance.

The East Side of Lauderdale

"Never mind why I'm here. I mean, okay, I spent the night in my office. I do that now and again. I heard a commotion and saw this guy hitting you. Who is this man, Jeff?"

"His name is Jed Peterson. He's one of the detectives on the abduction case. He … had a beef with me."

"I see." Sam knelt down and put an ear to Peterson's chest. "I'd better call nine-one-one."

"Okay," Bruce mumbled as Sam picked up a phone. He heard her report that a man had broken into her office, and she had been forced to defend herself. She urged that an ambulance be sent over immediately.

When she hung up, she turned to Bruce.

"You should go and leave it between him, me, and the police. It will be cleaner that way."

Bruce was befuddled.

"I don't know what to say, Sam. Thanks. Thanks for saving my life."

"You're welcome. Now you should really go. When the cops get here, it will be as simple as he broke in, and I happened to catch him."

Bruce shook his head, which made him even dizzier.

"Can't do that. I'm not going to leave you alone with this creep. He could come to and come after you. And you don't think he's going to tell the cops about me? He might tell them he thought I was breaking into this office and was trying to apprehend me. It would be a mistake to fib, Sam."

She seemed almost irritated.

"You don't need to be involved. Now go!"

"But I am involved," he insisted, sensing there was a distinct reason she didn't want him here.

"Listen, dammit—"

But then his eyes went beyond her. She whipped around and saw what he saw. An older man was standing in the darkened doorway of her office. He had gray hair, that was now tussled, and a goatee, and he wore only boxer shorts with a substantial belly protruding over them.

Bruce immediately recognized him: Joe Petruska, the former mayor and current publisher of the *East Lauderdale Tattler*. And then Bruce understood. Petruska and Sam had been here all night, probably on her couch. Her office must have been their love nest. Which made sense, considering Petruska was a married man and Sam still lived with her mother.

"What's going on out here?" Petruska asked in a sleepy grumble.

Sam turned to look back at Bruce, who raised an eyebrow. It was almost comical that she was carrying on a May-December relationship with the publisher. Bruce momentarily wondered if she did this willingly, or as a means to bolster her career. If it were the latter, it would explain how she had become an editor at such a young age.

Bruce breathed in heavily, starting to feel his footing come back.

"Don't worry, Sam. I won't tell anyone. But I do recommend you keep Mr. Mayor there out of sight, because police reports are public knowledge. And you should put on some clothes before the cops get here."

She looked down at her nearly naked body.

The East Side of Lauderdale

"Oh, my gosh. Thank you," she said quietly.

Then she walked past Bruce to Petruska.

"Dammit, Joe," she hissed and pushed the old man back into her office.

Soon, a parade of police and paramedics arrived, vehicle after vehicle with lights flashing, rolling into the *Tattler* parking lot. Sam jumped into the same light-green pantsuit she had worn the day before, just in time to greet the rescuers.

The police took statements from Bruce and Sam, who told the truth, aside from neglecting to relate that Sam had spent the night with Petruska, who managed to stay hidden. Meanwhile, the paramedics tended to Peterson, staunching his head wound. As Peterson was carried out on a stretcher, Bruce noticed he was moving his arms, indicating, at least, that he wasn't dead.

A sergeant-supervisor told Bruce there would be an investigation into what had happened here, but Bruce knew that no matter what, he and Peterson had unfinished business, that the enraged cop would come after him again. He just hoped he would be ready the next time.

The sun was coming up as the rescuers cleared the scene. Sam and Joe Petruska finally emerged from her office and left without saying a word to Bruce, who had been sitting quietly at his desk, computer off. Sam did, however, give him an apologetic look.

Completely alone, Bruce put his head, still aching from Peterson's beating, in his hands. He thought it ironic that, if Peterson hadn't attacked him, he might be heading north on Interstate 75 by now. But maybe Peterson had knocked some sense into him.

Because now running away didn't seem right.

*

The sun was up bright when Charlie Benson pulled into the Flight Standards District Office and parked his Ford Ranger. Bruce, who had been sitting in his car, got out and ambled over.

"Hey, Charlie."

As he got out of his pickup, Benson regarded Bruce for a moment.

"Knew I hadn't seen the last of you."

Bruce followed the FAA manager into the building, where Benson directed him to sit in his office while he grabbed two cups of coffee. Upon returning, he gave one to Bruce and sat in the chair behind his desk.

"What is it today? More flight plans?"

Bruce sipped the steaming brew and shook his head.

"Charlie, I need you to pull a rabbit out of a hat. I need to know exactly where that Boeing 737 landed the night it flew to Asheville."

"The one that canceled his instrument flight plan before landing?"

"Yes. Before you said that it could have landed at another airport nearby."

"Wherever it was, the airport would have to be pretty big to handle a plane that size. Thing needs five thousand feet of runway, maybe more."

Bruce sighed.

"Look Charlie, it's possible that plane was involved in the abductions of those women who have been in the

The East Side of Lauderdale

news lately. That's why I'm asking you to give me your best guess on where it might have touched down."

Benson's eyes widened.

"Really? The same five women that—"

"The same."

Benson sensed Bruce's urgency and rocked forward to hoist himself up.

"Let's see what we can do. Be right back."

He returned shortly with a large map and unfolded it on his desk.

"This is a Coast and Geodetic of the Asheville area, and it's very geographically accurate because it's basically a big aerial photograph."

Benson leaned over the map and Bruce took the liberty of getting up and standing beside him. Benson ran a finger around the Asheville area.

"Outside of the main airport, there's really nothing in the vicinity that looks big enough to accept a 737," the FAA man muttered. "What was the date that plane flew that night?"

"The seventeenth of October."

"Hang on. Be right back."

This time he returned with the computerized log of air traffic activity near the Asheville airport that night.

"According to this, he canceled IFR twenty-five miles south of Asheville," Benson observed. "Plane that fast, I doubt he flew another ten miles from that point. Otherwise, he'd risk knocking heads with slower, smaller aircraft."

"So, is there an airport twenty-five miles south of Asheville?"

Benson's finger kept running along the map. Finally, it stopped.

"Not twenty-five. But here's a strip that's about thirty miles to the south. And it's definitely big enough to handle a jet, about eight-thousand feet of runway."

"A commercial airport?"

"Doesn't appear to be," Benson said, taking a closer look. "I'm guessing it's private. It doesn't appear to have a control tower."

To confirm his suspicion, he pulled out a standard air map, technically called a Sectional. It distinctly showed airports that had control towers by blotching them in blue. Benson cross-referenced the two maps.

"This airport doesn't even show on the Sectional," he said. "I wonder if it's even been authorized for private use."

"So that could be it," Bruce said, feeling his heart rate increase.

"Could be. I don't see any other strips this long around Asheville."

He and Benson then looked at each other.

"Let me give you the exact longitude and latitude coordinates," Benson said. "With a good GPS, the authorities will have no problem finding that field."

Feeling a tinge of excitement, Bruce started to smile for no good reason.

"Thanks. I owe you a cigar."

*

Back in the newsroom, late morning, Bruce grabbed a copy of the *Tattler* from the backroom and went to his desk. Sam's office was empty and he guessed she was

The East Side of Lauderdale

too shaken to work. The five iron was back in its corner and he wondered if it had blood and hair on it.

What a bizarre scene a few hours earlier, he thought.

Bruce studied the front page, which had features on a high-society wedding and the opening of a grooming salon for cats.

Then he saw the photo on the bottom of the page.

Tucker had a startled, if not frightened, expression. Petrucco had a lecherous smile. The caption read, "*Fort Lauderdale Post* columnist Sheryl Tucker and businessman Frank Petrucco share a moment at the Opera Society's charity function Tuesday."

Bruce crinkled his nose. Something about the photo set wheels rolling. It wasn't so much Tucker's expression. It was the fact that she was pictured at all. She absolutely hated the *Tattler*. How could she have allowed this?

Working on a hunch, he compiled a list of names of the five abducted victims. Then he conducted a search of the *Tattler's* computerized archive.

And he discovered something astonishing. Every victim had been the subject of a feature in the Tattler, embellished with a photograph, or had been in a stand-alone photograph, like the one of Tucker and Petrucco.

He went a step further, comparing the date each victim was last seen with the date of publication of her respective photo. Here he found a consistent period of two days between the time a photo was published and the date each woman disappeared.

He looked again at the photo of Sheryl Tucker and Frank Petrucco.

And then he knew: Tucker was in serious trouble.

18.

Tucker sipped a glass of chilled Chardonnay as she sifting through documents from the Secretary of State's office, heaped into a pile on her desk. These listed the seven or eight companies that Petrucco owned in Florida, including a waste-management firm and a freight-truck operation. But the main one was his video-production company and its associated distribution outlets.

She hoped to find clues that Petrucco was dirty, doing something illegal. Then perhaps she could deliver the knockout blow, see him put away. But so far she had found nothing. Considering she had been poring over the reports for almost five hours, her eyes were red and her mental energies were waning.

Although it wasn't quite eight o'clock, the newsroom had already emptied, except for the copy desk people, who worked on the other side of the room into the wee hours of morning. She had sent Bloom home earlier, even though he had offered to keep her company. She needed the luxury of time to carefully examine Petrucco's portfolio—without feeling an editor's presence.

Because her door was open, she could hear the background hum of computers and the distant garble of newsroom television sets. Suddenly, she looked up, thinking she heard someone outside her office.

"Anyone there?"

Hearing no answer, she returned to sipping and perusing.

Among Petrucco's holdings were four hotels in Miami, a charter yacht, and a chain of electrical appliance stores. None of this was surprising. The man obviously had money. She guessed that a good chunk of his legal revenues were funneled into his video operation. It had to be expensive to secretly produce real rape videos—because every person involved faced the real risk of felony charges and had to be duly compensated.

She made notes of corporate officers and assets, planning to double-back on all of it. Then, shortly after nine o'clock, she decided to call it a night. Tomorrow, she would continue with a stronger conviction to tie Petrucco to the missing women. The obnoxious jackass would discover it wasn't smart to tell Sheryl Tucker that she either kowtows to him or gets hurt.

As she finished her wine, the phone rang. It was Detective Carlos Pena, his voice strangely low.

"Sheryl, I was wondering if we might get together for a chat tonight."

"You have information for me?"

"Maybe. But I was thinking more along the lines of a quiet drink, see where we are on things. You and me."

The East Side of Lauderdale

She exhaled.

"It's late, Carlos. So maybe isn't good enough. Either you have something for me or you don't."

There was silence on his end as he put together his words.

"Sheryl, the thing is, I really want to see you. I was hoping we might even meet at the Sheraton … perhaps get a room."

She let out a chuckle that actually was an exclamation of surprise.

"Jesus, Carlos. You're not very subtle."

"Hey," he said softly, "that's where all this is heading, isn't it?"

She was quiet, disturbed by this sudden change in tone. She might have been attracted to the man, but she wasn't about to become intimate with the lead detective on a case she was working.

"Maybe in your mind. In my mind, I'm still wondering why you told the *Tattler* first that five women were abducted. I looked kind foolish, saying there were only four."

"Sheryl, once again, I had nothing to do with that. The department had a leak, and I can assure you that said leak has been found."

"Really. Who was it?"

"Not at liberty to say. But this person has been dealt with."

"That's nice. But that doesn't mitigate the fact you were sitting on information and didn't let me in on it."

"At the time everything was too preliminary. I was afraid to give you information on Betty Sue Curtis because it might have been in error."

"That supposed to be an apology?"

"It's an explanation. Look, Sheryl, this is going in the wrong direction. I called to say what we both already know. You and I have chemistry. I know you feel it, too. All I'm saying is, let's get together and explore the feeling."

"I don't think so, Carlos."

Now his voice had an edge to it.

"What, you afraid to be with someone who could satisfy you? Or are you truly happy with that old basset hound you call a husband?"

A tingling sensation danced down her back. The usually understated, if not polite, Pena was coming on like gangbusters. She found his tone weird and threatening. It also was unsettling that he had looked into her personal life and apparently knew who her husband was.

"I'm hanging up now, Carlos."

"Sheryl, please. I'm sorry I came on strong. But I need to see you."

"Not tonight."

With that, she did hang up. She shook her head and stared at the phone, wondering what had gotten into the man. She sighed and neatly stacked all the Petrucco paperwork on a corner of her desk. Then she shut down her computer and locked her office.

As she headed down to the garage, she quickened her pace. She had a funny feeling that Pena wasn't going to take "no" so easily, and she could see him racing to the *Post* to intercept her.

Happily, her car was close to the elevator doors at the fifth level, where she had parked. As soon as she

The East Side of Lauderdale

got off the elevator, she walked briskly to the Porsche, jumped in and hit the automatic door lock. She looked around to see if she had been followed, but saw no one.

Giggling nervously at her paranoia, she fired up the engine and drove slowly down the garage ramp toward the exit. As she pulled onto the street, a white van started trailing her, and a maroon pickup followed behind the van.

19.

He dialed the Fort Lauderdale Post for a sixth time in two hours.

"Sheryl Tucker, please," he said, his irritation obvious.

"She's busy. Can I take a message?"

Bruce grimaced. The *Post's* newsroom night clerk, a young man, had obviously been ordered not to disturb Tucker.

"I've already left several messages."

"This Jeff Bruce, again?"

"Yes, it's Jeff Bruce. Again."

"I'll let her know you called."

"Listen, dammit. This is important. And I'm tired of getting the run-around."

"I'm sure you are."

"Hey, you little—" Then he caught himself. "Please. You've got to connect me. I have something extremely urgent to tell her."

"Right. What's your number again?"

The East Side of Lauderdale

Bruce spat out the number and slammed down the phone. He began to wonder why he should even try to warn Tucker, the woman who had gone out of her way to belittle him.

But he knew he had to. Time might be running short.

Because it was almost nine o'clock, he considered calling the police. If he explained the correlation between the victims and their photos appearing in the *Tattler*, they might attempt to contact Tucker.

But he knew how cops worked. A supervisor would want him to come in and chat extensively before acting on this type of information. Nothing would happen fast. He decided to drive to the *Post*, a good five miles away, to warn her in person.

*

There was a chill in the evening air as he ran out of the *Tattler* building to his car. He would need to move fast. Once Tucker left her newsroom, she would be unreachable because her home phone and address were tightly protected.

He barely had the key in the VW's door when he felt a hand on his shoulder. He whipped around fearing Jed Peterson had already recovered.

But Kasey stood there, clad in black jeans and a black sweatshirt, her hair pulled back severely into a ponytail. Even though she wore athletic shoes, he still had to look up to her.

"You certainly like to sneak up on people, officer."

"I have to tell you something."

He could see that she was upset and wanted to know why.

But time was of the essence if he was to get to Tucker.

"Listen, Kasey, before you tell me—"

"I've been reprimanded and I might be suspended."

"What? Why?"

"Jed identified me as the leak. After he was taken to the hospital, he told the commander that I stole the files from his desk and gave them to you. I'm sure it was payback for dumping him. Now I've have to explain myself in an administrative review next week, and if they don't like what they hear, they take away my gun and badge. At a minimum, I'll be blacklisted for any future promotions and urged to go job hunting. So much for becoming a detective."

"Christ," Bruce said quietly. "I'm sorry."

"You know what burns me? Carlos Pena, Jed's partner, gave sensitive information to the *Post*. But no one said a word to him. Me? I'm taking heat."

Bruce shook his head.

"I feel responsible, Kasey. You went out on a limb for me, and I don't blame you for being mad at me."

She took a step closer and he could see that her jaw was clenched. He wanted to take a step back as a precaution but already was up against his VW.

"I'm not mad at you, Jeff. I'm incensed with myself. And I think you should know why."

He looked at his watch. "I'd like to but—"

She put a hand up, and he reluctantly went silent.

"Please hear me out. Two years ago, I was in the middle of a hostage situation. Flying above it as a spotter, actually. All of the sudden, I see a guy appear on a roof with this old lady. I knew something was wrong, but I hesitated. I was like a deer staring at headlights—until I finally notice this guy has a high-powered weapon. But by the time I called the SWAT commander, the perp starts blasting away. He kills one officer and wounds two others. Then the perp blows away the woman, who just happened to be his mother, and then himself."

Bruce wrinkled his nose. He knew the story.

"That's a tough break."

"I was suspended but later found not culpable. Still, they wanted me to accept responsibility for my actions, or lack thereof. So I got moved to this late-night patrol, which was a severe demotion. In essence, they were hoping to humiliate me into quitting. I wanted to, but something happened."

"What?"

"Jed Peterson asked me out. At first he was a lifesaver, telling me to be strong and stick with the job because it needed people like me. He was supportive, and I needed that. So I ended up getting involved with him. But it wasn't long before I learned what a control-freak he is. He needed to know exactly where I was all the time, right down to who I was having lunch with. If another cop so much as made eyes at me, he suspected I was sleeping with the guy, and that usually ended with a fight."

"Like I said, he's a stalker," Bruce injected quietly.

"Stalker is probably a polite term for what he really is. But at the time, I welcomed his assertiveness because I was so down on myself. I only knew that it felt good to be with someone much stronger than me. Now I see things more clearly, and you helped me to do that."

"Me?"

"Yes. By working with you on this abduction thing, I noticed how you take a certain pride in yourself, in your work. That made me realize that I had no pride. I was wallowing in self-pity and enjoying it. But by giving you information, I started to feel better about things, like I was doing something really worthwhile. I actually started thinking again about trying to be detective someday. I began to see that Jed was part of my self-inflicted punishment for being a screw-up."

"I'm glad of that," Bruce muttered.

"Yeah, well, the problem is that now I'm back to going nowhere, now that I have two strikes against me. Seems like no matter how hard I try, I make one big mistake after another. I'm the loser, Jeff, not you. I'm so sorry for making those remarks to you last night."

Bruce saw the pain in Kasey's eyes. He knew she was pleading, not so much for forgiveness, but rather some kind of absolution.

"Let me tell you something," he said. "You've got all the right ingredients to be a great cop, if not a great detective. You've got a strong sense of right and wrong, and a passion to help people. If you give up, it will be a horrible waste of a great career. You need to fight this reprimand or suspension or whatever it is, and I'd like to help you. I'll talk to your commander and let him know that without you, this case wouldn't have seen the light of day."

The East Side of Lauderdale

Her eyes never strayed from his, but softened. She moved in close and put her arms around him. Then her mouth was on his.

20.

As she aimed home, Tucker tapped her steering wheel and sang to an old Rolling Stones tune on her radio, the one about not getting any satisfaction. It had grown chilly enough to turn on the heat, yet, per her habit, she drove with her driver's side window down, enjoying the smell of night air.

In truth, she had found a great deal of satisfaction. She was close to exposing Frank Petrucco for what he was—a felonious dirt bag. She wanted to be there when the cops slapped the cuffs on him, see his face as he was going down. Then she would chronicle Petrucco's journey to jail and finally leave Jeff Bruce in the dust, journalistically speaking.

She came to a stoplight on Andrews Avenue and sang more boldly.

"'Cause I try, and I ..."

Then she looked to her right and noticed a white van had pulled beside her. The man behind the wheel was leaning forward to leer at her.

The East Side of Lauderdale

She suddenly went quiet and prickles popped up on her forearms. She was used to men gawking at her while in traffic. They were easily ignored. But here she sensed serious danger in the dark.

Tucker continued tapping the wheel, only now nervously. When the light turned green, she gunned it. Because she was in a high-powered Porsche, she was able to leave the van behind quickly. A half a mile later, she didn't expect a maroon Ford pickup truck to spill out of a side street and ram into her rear-passenger side. The Porsche spun around and nearly rolled.

When it came to a halt on the side of Andrews Avenue, she was dazed. Then she saw red dripping onto her blouse. Her eyes moved to the rearview mirror, and she saw the open gash in her left temple. Her head had been knocked sideways into the car's door-frame.

Momentarily incapacitated, she could do little more than watch as the pickup pulled in front of her, while its young, stocky driver jumped out. He had a crewcut and a concerned look as he approached her rolled-down window.

"Are you all right, ma'am?"

Tucker tried to shake her head, no. But all she could do was gaze blankly at him.

He continued in a sincere Southern accent, "I am damn sorry about that, ma'am. I don't know what in the Sam Hill I was thinking."

Tucker opened her mouth to say something. But it was like she was drugged. Everything was bleary. And the pain in her wounded temple intensified.

The man leaned down and moved closer.

"Hey, your head's bleeding. Let's get you out of there and have a look."

Though dizzy and disoriented, Tucker had to presume the man had evil intent. She shook her head a bit, trying to come out of her malaise. The man opened her door and sternly grabbed her shoulder, attempting to pull her out.

As she groaned in resistance, the white van pulled behind her car. Seeing this second vehicle and that same leering driver, Tucker knew the collision was no accident. Adrenaline started pumping, and she managed to throw her sports car into first gear and floor it. The stocky man instinctively jumped back.

"Bitch!" he yelled. "Brad, go! Get her!"

*

Now the world quickly came back into focus. She was a fox being chased by baying hounds, and her life was on the line. As she sped south on Andrews Avenue, she caught a green light and crossed over State Road 84 into a dark, industrial, warehouse area near the airport. She immediately realized this was a mistake because her pursuers might catch her in a dead end.

And they were closing in fast, their headlights ever brighter in her rearview mirror. She flicked the electric switch to roll up her window and noticed her left hand was covered in blood, which continued to drip from the left side of her forehead.

She tried not to panic and strained to formulate a plan. She needed to loop back towards downtown and make it to the police station, where she could lose

The East Side of Lauderdale

these jerks. She figured they had to be associated with Petrucco.

Tires squealing, she made a sharp right turn onto a side street off Andrews. But a block later, the pickup suddenly pulled out in front of her. She slammed on the brakes and the Porsche skidded around to a stop, just short of a collision. The white van arrived to box her in, all in shadows because the nearest street light was fifty yards away.

The two men jumped out of their vehicles and jogged toward her car. Tucker stayed put, knowing if she ran they would catch her easily. At least with the windows up and doors locked, she had a modicum of protection. But she knew she they would try to kick in a window.

She felt around the passenger seat for her purse and cell phone. But in the commotion, the purse had fallen to the floor, and she couldn't waste time reaching down and finding it. She also sensed that a quick motion, such as leaning down, might cause her to faint; as she was becoming light-headed from blood loss.

The two men approached either side of her car, their foggy breath visible in the brisk night air.

"Get out of the car, ma'am, and I promise we won't hurt you," the taller and considerably skinnier of the two said.

Tucker locked eyes with him, remembering how he had been studying her intently when she first spotted him in the van at the traffic light.

Despite her terror, she gave him the finger.

"Up yours," she yelled.

She shoved the car into reverse and backed up hard into the front grill of the van. She heard the crinkling of bumpers and lights, as the van was pushed back a foot or two. With just a touch of room to maneuver, she put the Porsche in first and punched the gas. The skinny man hung onto her door handle and ran along for a few steps but quickly let go.

Because he was in her path, she tried to run down the stocky man with the crewcut. He dove out of the way as she side-scraped the pickup.

"She's not cooperating, Brad!" he yelled.

The two men ran to their vehicles.

*

Tucker found her way back to Andrews and charged north. After leaning over and groping around the floor, she got a hand on her purse. She yanked out her cell phone and started to dial 911.

But before she could push the last digit, the pickup rammed her Porsche so hard from behind that the phone flew out of her hand.

She screamed at the top of her lungs.

"No!"

She again hit the accelerator, downshifted and roared toward the intersection of Andrews and State Road 84. But the pickup hung close, its headlights and front grill filling her rearview mirror.

Suddenly, the traffic signal was right there: A red light.

Just yards ahead, cars whizzed through the intersection. She didn't even brake, but rather gunned it. Horns blared as she was nearly struck by two cars

The East Side of Lauderdale

and a delivery truck, which cut their wheels sharp and came to a stop.

But remarkably, she found herself on the other side of State Road 84, charging away, while her attackers were caught in the chaos she left behind.

She almost laughed.

In only blocks, she would make it to the police station.

But then her engine sputtered. And then it died.

"No! Dammit, no!" she yelled, seeing that her fuel gauge needle had settled on empty.

Because the car was in gear, it decelerated rapidly. She pulled the Porsche over to the right-side curb and stopped in front of Broward General Medical Center. She again felt around for her cell phone, taking precious seconds. But once she found it, she jumped out and started running.

The hospital would be almost as good as the police station. If she could just make it inside and find security guards or any other hospital personnel, she would be protected from these whackos.

She ran toward a sidewalk that led to the hospital's back parking lot and entrance. Along the way, she had intended to call 911 on her cell. But she got a wild hair and hit the speed-dial to Richard Bloom's home.

She needed him to know what was going on, not some dispatcher.

Putting the phone to her ear as she galloped, she heard one ring. Then the pickup screamed to a halt behind her car. And the driver was suddenly sprinting after her. Tucker yelped in surprise and tried to run even faster.

But now the blood-loss from the gash in her temple took its toll, and she was overcome with a bout of dizziness and exhaustion. She tried to keep running but felt like her feet had turned into lead. The man closed in like a cheetah on a small dog and dove for one of her ankles, tripping her up. She made it a point to fly onto some grass next to the sidewalk. She hit the ground and rolled.

The cell phone flew out of her hand.

"No!" she screamed again at losing her cellular lifeline. "No!"

Then he was on her. He grabbed her from behind and picked her up with astounding strength. He slapped an open hand over her mouth and nonchalantly carried her back toward the street while she kicked and squirmed.

The white van pulled up and the driver jumped out to open the cargo door. She was dragged inside and quickly subdued with a gag and shackles. One of the men, she wasn't sure which, took a moment to place a rag of some sort against her head to stem her bleeding. The rag was held in place with one wrap-around of thick, gray duct tape.

And then the hood was placed over her head, and the cargo door closed.

Looking around, seeing no apparent witnesses, the men got behind the wheels of their respective vehicles and drove calmly toward the airport, leaving Tucker's Porsche at the curb. Twenty minutes later, they carried her on board the Boeing 737. And twenty minutes after that, the jetliner's engines whined to life.

*

The East Side of Lauderdale

At his home with a vodka on ice in hand, Bloom stared at his phone. He thought he had heard Tucker yell. And he thought he had heard a ruckus. But it was so confusing that he wondered if it was a prank call.

21.

She pushed him back against his car, leaned into him, and squeezed him hard. Her kisses turned into bites, displaying a passion so powerful that she seemed angry, rather than aroused.

But Bruce wasn't about to protest. He was electrified. This was Officer Kasey Martin, tall, beautiful, exotic—his ultimate fantasy. He wished this first frenetic moment could last forever.

But he knew that it would have to end, fast.

He managed to pull his mouth away from hers.

"Wait a minute," he said between breaths.

That didn't stop her attack. She moved to his neck. He felt teeth and suction. Her nails clawed at his back over his shirt.

"Kasey, really, wait."

She stopped, puzzled.

"What? You don't like this?"

"Yes, of course I do. But I have to tell you something. Something important."

The East Side of Lauderdale

She pulled back defensively, frustration in her face.

"What?"

He put his hands on her shoulders.

"I didn't mean to spoil the moment, but I think Sheryl Tucker is in danger—serious danger. I was on my way to warn her when you intercepted me."

Kasey was befuddled.

"What kind of danger?"

As concisely as he could, he told her about the connection he had discovered, that all five of the missing women had been featured in the *East Lauderdale Tattler* with prominent photographs. Then each had disappeared not long after her picture was published. And now Tucker had been displayed in the *Tattler* that day.

Her reaction was to laugh.

"That's a stretch," Kasey said. "You think whoever abducted these woman is working off the *Tattler*? Why such an obscure publication? No offense."

"Maybe for that very reason. It's a small paper that gives high-society women extremely complimentary displays, even more so than the *Post*."

"Doesn't make much sense. But it might be worth calling the detectives tomorrow. Who knows? Maybe they'll get a subscriber list from the *Tattler* and—"

He put a hand up.

"I think Tucker is in trouble tonight. I don't think we have tomorrow."

Kasey stared at him.

"So what do you want to do?"

"Let's head to the *Post* and find her."

Kasey nodded, but was clearly disappointed that they were unable to finish what they had started.

*

They took her Jeep and raced south on the chronically congested Federal Highway. Yet Kasey made good time, changing lanes and speeding past a blur of car dealerships, insurance offices, and fast-food restaurants.

There was little talk along the way. She had the same serious demeanor as when she flew, and Bruce knew better than to distract her. But he couldn't help occasionally glancing at her, amazed at what had just happened. Suddenly, she looked back and smiled knowingly.

Ten minutes later, in the middle of downtown Fort Lauderdale, she brought the Jeep to a skidding halt by the *Post's* main entrance. Because this was a no-parking zone, one of the building's security guards immediately rushed over.

"Hey, move it along," he said gruffly.

Kasey flashed her badge and brushed past the guard.

"Get out of the way," she snarled.

Once inside, they took an elevator to the eleventh floor. She had to put her badge in another guard's face, this one behind a security desk.

"Where's the newsroom?" she demanded.

The guard pointed, and Kasey and Bruce charged.

A young man with a ponytail sat at the newsroom reception desk, reading a paperback. He didn't even look up as they galloped toward him.

The East Side of Lauderdale

"Hey!" Kasey yelled to get his attention. "Fort Lauderdale police. We need to talk to Sheryl Tucker—now."

The ponytail shrugged with an I-don't-give-a-damn attitude. He didn't like being harassed on the late shift.

"Not here," he said nonchalantly. "Gone for the night."

Bruce immediately recognized his voice as the one that had given him a hard time all afternoon. He wanted to grab the son of a bitch and shake him, but in the interest of time, he let Kasey do the talking.

"Then give me her home phone and address," Kasey commanded.

"No can do, ma'am. We have strict orders never to give out a staffer's home phone or address to anyone, including cops."

Kasey squinted.

"Listen, you little prick, I'm not playing games."

"I'm not either, officer," he said, although meekly. "I could get fired if I—"

The phone rang at his station.

"Okay if I get this?" he asked.

Kasey tried to say no, but he answered anyway.

"*Fort Lauderdale Post*. How can I help you?"

He listened to the caller, then looked up at Kasey and Bruce.

"She's not here, Richard. But there's a police officer standing right here, and she's looking for Sheryl, too. You want to talk to her?"

The ponytail addressed Kasey.

"I got Sheryl's editor here. He wants to talk to you."

Kasey instructed him to transfer the call to a nearby desk. After announcing who she was, she listened for a few seconds.

"Lay that on me again," she said sternly. "What happened, exactly?"

On the other end of the line, Richard Bloom cleared his throat.

"I got this very strange call, and I'm sure it was Sheryl. But all I heard was her yell, 'No!' Then there was … like this tussle. I think she might have been attacked somehow, unless she's playing some sort of practical joke."

"She tend to play jokes on you?"

"Never. The caller ID was definitely Sheryl. When I tried calling her back, her line was busy. I tried her at home and got the answering machine. That's why I called the newsroom."

"When's the last time you saw her, Mr. Bloom?"

"About six o'clock. I normally stick around while she's in there. But she said she had a lot of tedious paperwork and sent me home."

"What was she working on?"

"Another column about Frank Petrucco, how he is a major suspect in those abductions."

"So you don't know where she was headed after she left the newsroom?"

"I would think home. But again, I tried there. No luck."

"Can you give me her home address and phone?"

The East Side of Lauderdale

Without hesitation, Richard gave her the protected information.

"Okay, Mr. Bloom. Thank you. We're going to try to find her, but in the meantime, you should keep trying to reach her. If you do, give me a call."

She gave Bloom her cell phone number, and they hung up.

Kasey looked at Bruce.

"Sounds like you were right. She's in trouble."

Bruce nodded and looked around the *Post* newsroom. It reminded him of his former newsroom in Dallas: big, imposing and sophisticated. Then he saw the snotty young clerk staring at them impatiently.

"Let's get out of here," he said.

They were on the elevator, halfway to the ground floor when Kasey came close and kissed him again. Despite the tension arising from the Tucker situation, they kept at it well after the doors had opened.

After they stepped off, he said, "It would be a mistake to go to Sheryl's home."

"Why?"

"Because I'm pretty sure she's already on her way somewhere else."

*

At Bruce's urging, they raced toward Fort Lauderdale-Hollywood International Airport. Kasey again had her hands tight on the steering wheel. But now her mind was racing almost as fast as her Jeep.

She was debating whether to contact a commanding officer. This was a big case and she now had crucial information. First was the connection Bruce had found between the Tattler photos and the missing women. Then there was the call Bloom had received, giving credence to the possibility that Tucker might have been abducted.

But she hesitated, nonetheless.

She knew if she handed this off to the big boys, she would be immediately locked out. She wouldn't be allowed to participate in any way because of her reprimand. And she wanted badly to play some kind of role, if for no other reason than redemption for her past mistake—when she had failed to take immediate action. She decided that the immediate action needed in this case was to trust the man beside her. She turned and regarded Bruce, who was already looking back, seemingly knowing what she was thinking.

"It would be best for now if we try to get a better handle on what happened to Tucker before you call your superiors," he said.

She nodded.

From State Road 84, they took a back road to the north side of the airport and the Royal International compound. In the same parking lot where Bruce had done his so-called stakeouts, she parked the Jeep by a security fence. They jumped out and looked around.

The Boeing 737 was gone.

"Damn it," Bruce muttered.

"Where do you think it—?"

Then there was thunder above, and Bruce looked up.

"That's it," he said, pointing. "There it goes."

The East Side of Lauderdale

Kasey also looked up to see the familiar blue and white jet climbing into the cool, night sky, lights flashing all over its fuselage.

"You think Sheryl is on it?"

"I'd bet the bank on it." Bruce grabbed her hand. "Kasey, if I told you where that jet is heading, could you follow it in your helicopter?"

She furrowed her brow.

"Where's it going?"

"Asheville, North Carolina. Or, at least, not far from there. I can give you exact coordinates," he said, recalling his meeting with Charlie Benson.

Kasey frowned.

"That jet will be in Carolina in about two hours," she said. "It would take the JetRanger more than four, and that doesn't include a fuel stop—or two."

"But that's still a lot faster then trying to find a flight over at the terminal."

She looked down. He could tell she was tormented.

"Jeff, the proper protocol would be to call my commander, who would then notify the authorities in Asheville. The right thing would be to give the police in North Carolina those coordinates. Let them move in. If I take that helicopter, it would be an unauthorized flight. And I'm already in trouble with the Department."

He squeezed her hand harder.

"We could play it that way, Kasey. But I don't think any police agency is going to chase that jet without a lot of explaining first. I think we're dealing with some real bad people, and if we have any hope of saving Tucker, maybe the other women, we need to move right now. By tomorrow, Tucker could be dead."

Kasey swallowed, then nodded.
"Let's go."

22.

They again jumped in her Jeep and dashed north on Interstate 95 toward Fort Lauderdale Executive Airport.

"We'd best stop for some snacks," Kasey said, as she pushed her vehicle toward ninety miles per hour. "It's going to be a long night."

"Good idea."

They got off at Commercial Boulevard and screeched into a Seven-Eleven just beyond the interstate exit ramp. Inside, Kasey ran to the cold cases and grabbed three pre-wrapped ham and cheese sandwiches and four bottles of cold water. Bruce picked up a large bag of potato chips and a box of powdered donuts. At the cash register, he pulled out his wallet, anxious to pay. But a foreign-national cashier took his time ringing up the items—until Kasey leaned at him.

"Step it up, dammit," she yelled in his face.

Three other people in the store looked up, wondering if a robbery was in progress.

"Okay, okay, lady, don't split a gut," the rattled man said.

Rather than wait for change, Bruce threw twenty-five dollars at the wide-eyed man, which was five more than the food was worth. They charged back to the Jeep, and Kasey threw the snack bag in the back. Then she roared out of parking lot and accelerated all the way to the entrance to the general aviation airport, about a mile from the convenience store.

Parking haphazardly next to the police compound hangar, Kasey retrieved some cold-weather gear and her Glock 9mm from the back of the Jeep, while Bruce fetched the snacks. She ran into the office and lifted the keys to a helicopter. Ten minutes later, she had a chopper ready to go.

As they had done on their first flight together, Bruce took the left seat while she settled into the right. She coaxed the turbine engine to life, and they put on their headsets.

"The coordinates," she said into the aircraft's intercom, voice edgy.

Bruce pulled out his notebook and showed her the longitudinal and latitudinal information. She plugged the numbers into the cockpit's GPS, hoping they led to a private airport in North Carolina and six abducted women, now with Tucker in the mix. Then she boosted the throttle and eased the JetRanger into the air.

It rose ten feet, its landing light burning bright on the ramp, navigation lights blinking, and rotor blades whomping on an otherwise peaceful night.

"This is absolutely crazy," she muttered to herself, though Bruce heard it.

The East Side of Lauderdale

"But absolutely necessary," he said evenly, catching her eye.

She held his stare for a moment, then nodded.

"I know. I'm just nervous."

He nodded.

"Me, too."

She pushed the controls to progress forward. But as she did so, a motorcycle roared out of the darkness, though she didn't immediately see it.

*

Much like a movie stuntman, its driver made a perilous leap off the bike and grabbed hold of the right-side skid.

The rider-less Harley Davidson then slammed into the side of the police aviation hangar. It crunched, bounced back, and exploded.

Kasey saw the explosion and felt the weight. But she didn't realize a man was hanging onto her aircraft until she looked down.

There was Jed Peterson, looking up at her, crazed with rage. He was pulling himself up toward the cockpit, fighting for footing. He had a white bandage wrapped around his head where Sam had whacked him.

Her first inclination was to put down to prevent Peterson from getting hurt. But before she could do so, he was suddenly standing on the skid outside her window. He popped the latch, opened the door, and jabbed an arm in. She didn't have the time or the room to dodge, and his long, thick fingers quickly found her throat.

He was finally taking his revenge, reckoning all the pain both Kasey and Bruce had caused him. She couldn't know it, but Jed's intention was to kill all on board, including himself.

"Lousy, fucking bitch!" he shrieked.

Both of her hands instinctively came off the controls, trying to pry his hand from her neck. But he was too powerful and determined. Kasey tried to scream, but the grasp was suffocating. Her legs flailed and her left knee inadvertently jammed the throttle in, prompting the turbine engine to surge and JetRanger to climb sharply. Items in the rear compartments shifted and clanged.

"If I can't have you, nobody can!" Peterson screamed above the roar.

At first Bruce was stunned, observing the attack as though it was in slow motion. But when he felt the chopper rise sharply, he reacted. His hands joined Kasey's in struggling to pull Peterson's fingers free from her throat.

But it was like trying to unravel a python.

"Son of a bitch! Let her go," Bruce cried out futilely.

Kasey started to make gurgling sounds, and her eyes were popping, while the helicopter continued ascending at more than a thousand feet per minute. It was also starting to lose momentum and control.

"If I can't fuck you, nobody can, least of all that little prick!" Peterson shouted, eyes wildly aiming at Bruce.

"Jed! Don't do this!" Bruce yelled.

The East Side of Lauderdale

Peterson responded with an eerie high-pitched yowl.

"Fuck you!"

Bruce pounded on Peterson's forearm with the bottom of his fists.

"Dammit! You're going to kill us all!"

"That's the idea, asshole!"

Kasey was on the verge of passing out and the helicopter was on the brink of falling out of the sky, its nose now at a perilously steep angle. The ground was no longer visible from the cockpit, only a mat of serene stars straight above.

Knowing he had seconds, fighting the pull of gravity, Bruce unsnapped his seatbelt. He pulled his knees to his chest to clear his legs of the close-quarters instrument panel. Then he took aim at Peterson's chest and kicked.

The big man grunted as he was jolted backwards. He almost lost his footing, but was able to cling to the door. He re-found his balance with a vengeance, pulling out his sidearm and pointing it at Bruce's head.

"You really know how to piss a guy off!" Peterson howled.

Bruce ducked as the first shot rang out, piercing the right-side window, wind immediately whistling through a small hole, surrounded by a spider web of tiny cracks. Bruce thought he felt the bullet buffet his pant leg as it ricocheted.

"Can't keep a bad man down!" Peterson bellowed. "Let's all take a ride to hell!"

Knowing the next shot wouldn't miss, Bruce reacted purely on instinct. He planted his feet against the lower left side of the cockpit for leverage, lunged over Kasey and rammed his right shoulder into the right-side door.

The door and all of Bruce's weight flew into Peterson's upper chest.

Peterson's left hand, which had been holding onto the outside latch, jerked loose. He stumbled, and his feet slipped off the landing skid.

He fought for balance. He screamed. And then he fell free.

As he plummeted and squirmed in the glow of the chopper's landing light, shots rang out harmlessly from his gun.

Bruce almost followed him because his momentum carried him halfway out the door. But he put a hand down, grasped the skid and stopped himself.

But by then, the aerodynamics keeping the helicopter aloft ran out of energy, and the aircraft nosed down abruptly into a tumbling spin.

*

Bruce battled against centrifugal force to resettle back into the cockpit.

He ignored the roller-coaster sensation of free-fall, grabbed Kasey's shoulders and shook her hard, back and forth, hoping to rattle some blood into her brain.

"Kasey!" Bruce screamed. "Come on, babe! Come to!"

Feeling the chopper careening downward, she moaned and clawed upwards through the grogginess. She forced herself to put her hands on the controls, reduce power, and push the nose forward. The craft

The East Side of Lauderdale

dropped even faster. But then, it stopped twirling as it regained critical airspeed. At five hundred feet above the ground, seconds from impact, Kasey took back full control.

Bruce pulled her door closed, fell back into his seat, and closed his eyes.

"You all right?" he asked, heart thumping.

Kasey also was breathing hard, holding her bruised neck with one hand and controlling the chopper with the other. She stared straight ahead and didn't respond for several seconds.

Then, in a near whisper, she rasped, "We need to go back and alert my squad. We need to find Peterson's body and—"

Bruce sat forward and looked into her glazed eyes.

"We can't do that, Kasey, not if we're going to save Tucker. As horrible as that was, we need to move along and leave it behind."

Kasey kept staring ahead. But several seconds later she nodded. She put the helicopter into a steady climb and accelerated forward.

*

It was more than an hour before either one said a word, each trying to deal with a whirlwind of emotions after Peterson's insane attack. A journey that started out tense was even darker now, and full of trepidation.

Kasey tried to settle down by methodically monitoring the cockpit gauges. Bruce found some medical tape in the emergency kit and plugged the bullet hole in the window to stop the incessant whistling.

Then he pulled out the snack bag.

"I'm starved," he said. "Being ambushed always gives me an appetite."

She looked at him stone-faced for a moment, then softened.

"Me, too. Pass me one of those sandwiches."

The food brought a sense of ease as the night plodded into the wee hours. As they flew northward at three thousand feet, following Florida's East Coast, both eventually refocused on the original mission. They made fuel stops in Jacksonville, on the north end of Florida, and in Columbia, South Carolina. In both places, they took time to shake off the vibration of the helicopter, down some coffee and use restrooms.

Then they braced to find their target.

Just before lifting off from Columbia, Kasey double-checked her air map. They would approach the private strip south of Asheville in less than an hour, and it was almost four a.m. Despite deep fatigue, she wanted to put down near the strip before first light if the element of surprise was to work in their favor.

"We need to be very careful about where we land," she said. "It can't be too close or they'll hear us. But we don't want a long hike, either."

Bruce nodded his acknowledgment.

As they flew northwest, the land became thick with forest and rolling hills, and because there was no moon, the world turned black. Soon the hills became low-level mountains, part of the Smokies, prompting Kasey to climb to seven thousand feet. Meanwhile, it was becoming increasingly colder, though the chopper's heat kept them comfortably warm.

The East Side of Lauderdale

When they were thirty miles out, according to the GPS, Kasey turned off the exterior lights, knowing the JetRanger could be seen for miles. She also slowed so that the engine wouldn't be quite as loud.

Bruce spotted the runway first.

"There it is," he said quietly. "Five to seven miles at one o'clock."

Kasey squinted.

"More like four miles. And there's your 737."

She dimmed the cockpit lights to get a better read on the outside terrain and brought the helicopter to a hover. She searched the ground for a flat landing spot. Bruce pointed down at something on his side.

"There's some sort of trail and an open area right there."

"Got it."

She eased toward it, aware that telephone wires or other obstacles could be hidden in the darkness. When she was right over the area, she turned on the landing lights and let down. The touchdown was smooth enough, and she immediately shut down the engine. Studying her surroundings, Kasey realized they had settled on a turnabout area on the side of a mountain road.

"We're about two miles away," she said. "Did you see that lodge, or whatever it was, next to runway?"

"That must be where they've got Tucker. Maybe the others."

"We need to move quickly and get there before dawn. You up to it?"

"I hope." Then he leaned over and kissed her gently. "You did good, getting us in here like that."

223

"Thank you," she said, and pulled him close to kiss him much harder.

*

The moment they opened the doors, they were assaulted by the raw cold. Kasey went to the chopper's back compartment, pulled out her police jacket, and threw a sweatshirt at Bruce. She also grabbed her gun and secured it into an underarm holster.

"Jesus. It's got to be about twenty degrees," he said, hopping around.

"More like fifteen. We move at a fast clip, we stay warm."

Being a well-conditioned athlete, she took off at a near-sprint.

"Hey," he called, but not too loudly. "Not *that* fast."

She slowed to an easy trot, and he strained to stay with her. It didn't help that he was wearing street shoes, while she had the luxury of running shoes. Meanwhile, the road sloped up and down, and was full of ruts and patches of ice. They still arrived at the runway area in less than thirty minutes, initially hiding behind a large, spindly pine to survey the scene. They saw no evidence of elaborate perimeter security.

"This is weird," Kasey whispered. "If any of those women are here, you would think this place would be guarded by everything from cameras to dogs."

"Maybe the security is in the lodge," Bruce said between gulps of air.

"Or it's invisible, like laser beams. Stay behind me. And stay close."

The East Side of Lauderdale

She unsnapped her firearm from its holster and kept it low by her side.

As they crossed onto the airfield property, Kasey expected to hear alarms and see bright lights. But they were able to pad quietly to the lodge, which had a surprisingly large ramp area, where the jetliner was parked.

Upon closer inspection, Kasey guessed that the lodge was ironclad. She could see the steel bars over the upper windows. From lightly tapping one of the lower windows, the timbre told her that they were made of something like Plexiglas, and likely bulletproof. Breaking in would be nearly impossible.

"You were right," she whispered. "This place is like Fort Knox."

"So," he said, teeth clacking as he shivered, "what do we do?"

"I say we wait until someone comes out," she said, pointing to the lodge's front double doors. "Then I put a gun to their head."

"Sounds like a great plan. Except, if they don't come out in the next twenty minutes, one of us is going to be dead of hypothermia. And that would be me."

She giggled in a nervous reaction to the dangerous position they were in.

"You got a better idea?"

He nodded.

*

As first light appeared on the eastern horizon, Brad prepared to hit the sack. It had been a long night, and his final chore had been to secure the 737. It had been

Ray's job to secure Sheryl Tucker. Which made Brad smile. Tomorrow, they would have lots of fun with her, and make her pay for being such a major-league bitch on the way up here.

He started to trudge up the stairs to his bedroom when he heard the raucous knocking. He looked at his watch. It was 5:30 a.m.

"What the—?"

He ran down to a control console area off the lobby and checked the security monitors, showing various views around the property. From these, he could see the man standing on the front porch, pounding on the front doors and hopping foot to foot.

Brad grabbed his silencer-equipped .38 from a tabletop and crept to the front door. Turning on the front porch lights, Brad studied the man through a slit in the curtains over the front door windows. He didn't appear to be the law.

"Hey," Bruce was yelling. "Anyone home?"

Brad pulled back the curtain and stared at Bruce, keeping the gun down.

"Can you help me out?" Bruce yelled to him. "I was driving to work on the road over there, ran out of gas, and well, it's damn cold out here."

Brad whipped open the door and grabbed Bruce by the collar with one hand and put the pistol to his head with the other.

"That's a private road with an impenetrable access gate. So you sure as hell didn't drive in. You FBI? Because I like to castrate FBI guys."

Bruce smiled meekly.

"Avon lady?"

The East Side of Lauderdale

Brad felt the gun to the back of his head and heard the click.

"Move and you're dead," Kasey said quietly.

23.

The man with short-cropped blond hair and a goatee slowly raised his hands, the firearm remaining in the right one.

"Easy, easy," he said cautiously. "Don't do anything crazy."

Kasey jammed the barrel of her Glock into the back of his neck. They were standing on a concrete porch under bright security lamps.

"Fort Lauderdale police. What's your name, mister?"

"Brad. Brad Holman."

"Well, Brad Holman, you must be pretty smart for a kidnapper. I ran your name through the FBI crime database and you came out clean."

He chuckled quietly.

"Smarter than most cops, anyway."

She jabbed him harder, and he winced.

"Not this time, you piece of dirt. Now slowly put the gun down on the ground. Make a move and I splatter your brains. Understand?"

"Perfectly, officer."

The East Side of Lauderdale

The sun began peeking over the pine-covered hills, and a smoky scent filled the air. Brad bent over slowly, lowering the gun. Kasey, her breath turning into clouds in the chilled air, kept her sidearm aimed at the back of his head. He dropped his weapon gently on the porch's surface.

"Now kick it away."

He started to move his foot. But then he swiftly reached back between his legs. The light was just dim enough that Kasey didn't immediately pick up this motion. Suddenly, she felt his hands grip her ankles.

"No!" she yelled, instead of firing a bullet into his skull.

He yanked hard and she collapsed backwards, falling on her hind end, her 9mm flying out of her hand and rattling across the tarmac. She immediately kicked free of his grasp and crawled desperately toward her gun.

But by then, Brad had picked up his gun and whipped it around. He pointed it at Kasey, who stopped only inches short of reaching her firearm. Brad motioned for her to stand up. As she slowly did so, he stepped toward her with a twisted grin. Then he crisply backhanded her.

She cried out in pain, putting her hands to her face.

"Call me dirt," he muttered.

Then Brad heard the footsteps. He pivoted to see Bruce charging with arms outstretched, like a linebacker trying to sack a quarterback. Brad raised the .38, the silencer fat over the barrel. Bruce could have stopped. But he kept going.

Full speed ahead.

Brad smiled.

Kasey yelled, "No!"

Brad fired. Rather than the loud report, the sound was soft and deadly, like dart penetrating a beanbag. Bruce felt the lead slice through his upper right leg, a hot sensation followed by piercing pain. Blood immediately spurted.

Bruce recoiled, leaned down, and grabbed at the wound.

But he kept moving in Brad's general direction.

Brad fired again, this one penetrating Bruce's upper chest.

"No!" Kasey yelled again.

Bruce fell to the ground, rolled over onto his stomach, and lay still.

Kasey started to run to him, but Brad aimed his gun at her with a two-handed stance.

"Stay away from him!"

She stopped, staring at Bruce then turning to Brad.

"Bastard! You bastard!"

Brad again broke into an off-kilter grin, one of his front teeth slightly crooked. Keeping the .38 on her, he went to Bruce and cautiously kicked the body over. Satisfied he was dead, Brad glared at Kasey.

"I should kill you on the spot. But I think I'll have some fun first."

*

The East Side of Lauderdale

Inside, Brad's muscle-bound partner, Ray, stood behind the door, his gun at the ready. Wearing only underwear, Ray inquired, "What the hell?"

Brad pushed Kasey in front of him into the lodge's front foyer.

"Just some bitch cop."

"Cop? Christ, Brad, I thought you said they'd never find the place."

"Don't sweat it. She and the dead guy out there came alone."

"You sure?"

"If there was backup, they'd be here already. Now let's go unwind a bit. We'll do this bitch then that other bitch and put them both on the same video. Our customers will love it."

Kasey tensed.

"You're going to make a video? With me?"

Brad chuckled.

"Not just any video: a very exclusive video for a very exclusive clientele. Our clients pay a hundred thousand a pop to see bitches like you get what they deserve. The fact that you're a cop should make the production all the more, shall we say, marketable? So guess what. You're going to be a star. Ray, pat her down, make sure she isn't carrying another gun."

"My pleasure."

Ray groped every part of her, which she endured with gritted teeth. He found her cell phone and threw it on a tabletop. Putting his gun barrel against her back, Ray marched her upstairs, Brad close behind.

They shoved her inside a bedroom, and she froze with terror.

There was Tucker, naked, each of four limbs tied tightly to one of four bedposts. She had a fishing bob in her mouth, forcing her jaws wide open, and the bob was kept in place with fishing line that wound several times around her head. She had the wild eyes of a trapped animal and a red sore, with no bandage, on her left temple from the earlier car crash.

In front of the bed was the big video camera on its tripod.

Seeing Kasey's alarm, Brad pointed his gun in her face.

"If you're a good girl, do exactly as you're told, we'll let you live. Now strip."

She nodded, as though totally resigned, and slowly pulled off her police jacket. But he made the mistake of glancing at Tucker, and Kasey lunged, swiping the gun out of his hand. She clubbed him once with a fist to the side of his face before Ray grabbed her from behind.

"No!" she screamed and kicked.

He put her in a reverse bear hug and lifted her off her feet.

"Spunky little bitch, isn't she, Brad?"

Brad, holding the side of his head, said, "Yeah, spunky. Put her down."

Ray did so, and Brad slapped her again, so hard that her head snapped around. She went limp and fell to the floor.

"Get a chair and tie her up, Ray."

Ray retrieved a chair and sturdy rope from downstairs while Brad ripped off Kasey's shirt and pants, leaving her in a bra and panties. It would be sexier that way when the tape started rolling, he thought. The

The East Side of Lauderdale

two men positioned her on the chair and tied her arms behind its back and her ankles to the two front legs.

"Damn, she's got a nice body," Ray observed.

"An athlete's body," Brad added. "This is really going to be hot."

Both kept leering at her as they stripped down. Outside the bedroom window, the sun rose higher into the morning sky, turning the hills a vivid, dark green, and the sky a cobalt blue. Some of the sunlight seeped into the room and found Kasey's closed eyes, her head hanging down, bands of hair dangling.

"Okay, Ray, turn on the video. We'll double-team this one first."

Ray hit the record button, the lens capturing Kasey in the foreground and Tucker in the background, watching in horror, knowing she was next.

Just as the men were about to start on her, Kasey opened her eyes slightly, raised her head and asked, "Who's the head of this operation?"

She wanted to know who to kill if she survived.

"No harm telling you now," Brad said. "Clayton McGreggor's the top man."

Tucker let out a muted scream behind her gag. Clayton McGreggor, her good breakfast buddy, had set her up for this.

Kasey also seemed surprised, despite her stupor.

"What about this guy Petrucco?"

"Small potatoes," Ray said. "He jumps at Clay's command."

The two men laughed before Brad addressed Kasey sternly.

"Enough small talk. If you resist in any way, I am going to stick a knife in your eye. Got it?"

"Yes," she whispered.

He moved closer while Ray kneeled in front of her. Ray started to peel down her panties as two shots rang out.

Ray looked bewildered before he fell over, his face falling in Kasey's lap.

Brad staggered for a step with just enough life left to turn and see who had killed him. Then he fell onto his stomach at Kasey's feet.

Both had gunshot wounds to the back of the head.

Bruce stood at the doorway, holding Kasey's smoking gun, the Glock 9mm she had left on the ramp by the plane. He limped to Kasey, grabbed Ray by the hair and pulled him off her. The big body slammed backwards onto the floor.

"Jeff," she said in soft amazement.

"It's going to be all right, Kasey."

He was able to untie her arms before he collapsed.

24.

Kasey tore the rope from her ankles, sprang up, and freed Tucker.

"Filthy pigs," Tucker grumbled, spitting out the fishing bob. "They died too easy."

She rolled off the bed and found her dress on the floor, where her captors had ripped it off her the night before. Kasey pulled on her jeans and sweatshirt. Both women rushed to Bruce, who had lost an enormous amount of blood and was laboring to breathe.

"He's going into shock," Kasey said.

She went to the bedroom's clothing chest, rummaged through the drawers, and found two white-cotton nightgowns. She unbuttoned Bruce's shirt and pressed one against his chest wound. The other was wrapped around his oozing upper leg. Tucker grabbed a pillow from the bed and put it under his head.

The two women knelt on either side of him. Kasey knew he needed to be taken to a hospital immediately.

"Sheryl, did you see any other women here?" she asked, as she tightened the makeshift tourniquet on Bruce's leg.

"No. They took me right up here last night. If you hadn't come when you did, that guy was going to—"

She shut her eyes tight and grimaced.

Kasey reached over and put a hand on her shoulder.

"Stay with Jeff, keeping holding this shirt against his chest while I call for help. Then I need to check the rest of this place."

Tucker nodded and took over applying pressure to slow the bleeding.

Before she went, Kasey took Bruce's hand. It was cold.

"Hang on, Jeff. Help will be here soon. Okay?"

"Sure," he whispered, with eyes half-shut.

Then he squeezed her hand slightly. She bit back tears and got up. She found her gun where Bruce had dropped it after killing Brad and Ray.

Racing down the stairs, Kasey found her cell phone on the counter where she had seen Ray toss it. She made the emergency call, knowing it would bring a swarm of police and rescue workers—and likely the end of her career. She had violated numerous protocols, not the least of which was failing to call for backup. But none of that mattered with Bruce in dire condition and a handful of women probably imprisoned somewhere in this old lodge.

Identifying herself as a police officer, Kasey told a dispatcher there had been a shooting. To provide a location for the lodge, she gave the longitudinal and

The East Side of Lauderdale

latitudinal coordinates that had been inserted into her helicopter's GPS.

Then she set out to search for five women, hoping they were still alive.

*

Holding the Glock in front of her, on the off-chance more than two perpetrators were involved, she padded quickly around the first floor. She crossed through the lobby, a banquet room, and the kitchen and saw nothing unusual. She found a bedroom wing with doors open and rooms vacant. But then, returning to the lobby, she noticed another staircase across the way. She made her over to it, sweeping the gun in every direction as she went. She cautiously climbed the wooden stairs, which creaked with each step. At the top she was greeted by another hallway full of bedrooms.

This time, all the doors were closed. Coming to the first one on her left, she tried to twist the old-fashioned knob and found it locked. She knocked.

"Police," she called out. "Anyone in there?"

There was no answer. But she thought she heard groaning. She pressed her ear to the door for a better read and could tell someone was inside. Kasey felt her heart thump into gear.

"Back away from the door!" she yelled.

She fired at the lock, aiming down and away. The door swung open.

A woman crouched in the corner let out a startled yelp. Quivering, keeping her eyes down, she had her arms wrapped around her body in a defensive posture.

She wore only panties. Her face was ravaged with red blisters.

"Please don't touch me," she begged, voice hoarse and weak.

Kasey came closer.

"I'm with the police, ma'am. I'm not going to hurt you."

The woman cautiously peered up at Kasey. She had hollowed eyes and gaunt cheeks, signs that she had eaten little and endured terrible trauma. From photographs, Kasey knew this was Melinda Norman.

"My God," Kasey whispered.

But there was an immediate jolt of hope. If Melinda Norman was alive, then maybe so were the others. Kasey pulled the top blanket off the bed, gently wrapped it around the distraught woman, and guided her to sit on the bed.

"Help is on the way, Melinda," Kasey said soothingly.

"Where are they?" Melinda Norman said, eyes darting in all directions.

"The two men?"

She nodded anxiously.

"They hurt me. God, they hurt me. They sprayed me with my own Mace while they were …"

"They can't hurt you anymore," Kasey assured her. "But I need to know, were there more than two of them?"

Melinda Norman cast tired, yet terrified, eyes down.

"Not that I saw."

The East Side of Lauderdale

"Are there other women on this floor? In the other rooms?"

"I think so." Her voice was barely audible.

"Stay here for now, okay? I'll come back to get you."

Melinda Norman didn't respond. She kept looking down.

*

After blasting off another lock on the next door down, she found Betty Sue Curtis, the cable television personality, who, upon seeing a woman instead of two male attackers, ran to Kasey and hugged her.

"Thank God," she repeatedly whimpered, with her face buried in Kasey's shoulder. "My husband. Can I call my husband? My children, I want to see my children!"

Kasey wrapped a blanket around her, as she, too, had on only underwear.

"In just a little while, okay? Right now we need to make sure everyone else is safe. More police will be here shortly. Then they'll contact your husband."

"But I need to—"

"Please, sit on the bed for now," Kasey said, directing her. "What happened to your clothes?"

Betty Sue Curtis winced.

"They gave me a wardrobe, the exact same outfits I wore to work. But with each attack they would rip off the clothes, shredding them ... until I had nothing."

"How many attacks were there?"

Betty Sue's face contorted into a mask of pain, holding back tears.

"Several," she muttered.

"They're dead now, Mrs. Curtis. They got what they deserved."

Betty Sue Curtis shook her head slowly, jaw tight.

"They'll never get what they deserve."

Kasey let that sink in a moment.

"Stay here. I'll be back soon."

"Hurry back," Betty Sue said quietly. "Please."

Kasey continued down the hall. She wished she didn't have to shoot the locks. But the doors were locked from the outside so the women couldn't open them from the inside. She yelled another warning and blew off a lock.

She found a naked Charlotte Baker waiting for her with a cocked arm and a hard fist, planning to slam the next person who came at her. Baker had heard the gunshots and didn't know what to expect.

When she saw Kasey, she screamed, "Who the hell are you?"

"I'm the police, ma'am. Please back down. I'm not going to hurt you."

Charlotte Baker, once a beautiful, graceful woman, now looked ten years older than her actual age. She stared at Kasey then fell back on the bed and began sobbing. Kasey wrapped a blanket around her and proceeded to the next room.

There she found Mary Sims huddled in her bed, under a blanket.

"Hey," Kasey coaxed. "It's the police. You can come out from under there."

The East Side of Lauderdale

Peeking out at Kasey, the tortured woman curled up and cried. When Kasey sat on the bed, Mary Sims sat up and hugged her.

"They just wouldn't leave me alone," she whispered, sniffing. "They always had that camera. Always the two of them. And they made me do horrible things."

"It's over now," Kasey said, rocking her.

Sims would be the last woman Kasey would find alive.

The next room was filled with the stench of death, and Kasey knew she was too late. She discovered Janice Weslowski, once the proud president of a Fort Lauderdale electronics firm, in the bathtub, wrists slashed with shards from a smashed perfume bottle. Because there was virtually no decomposition, Kasey guessed she had died within the previous forty-eight hours, a suicide.

That even one woman had perished at the hands of those monsters made Kasey's blood boil. But she forged on to be sure there were no others.

After twenty more minutes of going around the lodge, Kasey was convinced she had accounted for all the victims. She made another quick check of the four who were alive to ensure they had stayed put. Then she ran back to the wing where Jeff Bruce lay in critical condition.

Tucker was still holding the now blood-drenched nightgown to his chest.

"He's going downhill, fast," she said.

Kasey kneeled down and took Bruce's hand.

"Just keep hanging on, okay?"

Bruce could only gaze at her. He didn't have the strength to squeeze.

*

The sirens and whooshing helicopter blades could be heard miles away, bearing an army of law enforcers and fire-rescue workers, charging toward the lodge in the nether regions of western North Carolina. As the SWAT team flooded in the front door, automatic weapons at the ready, Kasey held up her badge and told them she had cleared the building. She pointed them toward the hallway where the women were still cowering.

"Be gentle," Kasey warned a SWAT commander. "They're all traumatized."

The paramedics came in right behind the police, and Kasey directed them to the bedroom where Bruce lay in a growing pool of blood. Within minutes, he was strapped to a gurney in preparation to be airlifted to an Asheville hospital. She wanted to accompany him, but she knew she needed to remain here at the scene. She would have squeezed his hand one last time, but the paramedics rushed him out too quickly.

After watching Bruce's helicopter fly away, Kasey returned to the lodge lobby, where she found Tucker, sitting on a couch with a blank look. Kasey sat beside her, and the two watched as the abducted women were taken, one by one, out on stretchers, placed on rescue vans, and transported to the hospital, where they would be treated initially as rape victims.

"You should go to the hospital, too," Kasey said quietly.

The East Side of Lauderdale

"I'm all right," Tucker said. "Just need to catch my breath."

"Okay, if you say so."

Both sat quietly for a moment, and then Tucker doubled over and wept, face in hands, with loud, sorrowful sobbing.

Kasey put an arm around her and suddenly found herself crying as well.

*

In time, more waves of law enforcement arrived, including the FBI and federal marshals. A team of investigators took preliminary statements from Kasey and Tucker to get a general picture of what had just happened here. Both were told they could expect a more thorough debriefing later.

Then the federal law enforcers focused on the Boeing 737. Because the main door wasn't locked, they gained easy access and found nothing unusual in the cabin. But upon examining the plane's lower cargo compartment, they discovered dozens of boxes of videos, featuring the rapes of the abducted women, ready to be mass-produced and sold on the black market.

They also came upon a crate shaped like a casket. After the crate was removed from the aircraft and pried open, investigators found Commissioner Sidney Simon inside, with a single bullet wound in the middle of his forehead. He was in the same business suit he had worn the morning he had tried to warn Tucker to stay clear of this whole mess. And it later would be determined that he had been murdered by a bullet that came from Brad Holman's silencer-equipped .38 semiautomatic.

When federal officials informed Tucker about Simon, she was still camped out in the lodge lobby, holding a cup of steaming coffee, still shell-shocked by all that had happened. But now she sagged, overcome with profound sadness and guilt. She had been the one to expose the commissioner as one of Petrucco's porn customers. And she guessed that, once that was in the open, Clayton McGreggor, the man in charge of this incredibly disgusting operation, had ordered the hit, fearing Sidney would go to the police.

Despite everything that had happened, Tucker knew what she had to do. She was a journalist above all else, and the discovery of the five women, how they had been victims of a horrible scheme, how one had taken her own life, and how the Broward County Commission chairman had been murdered; all combined to make earth-shattering news.

She put down the coffee, borrowed a mobile phone from one of the officers, and called Richard Bloom in Fort Lauderdale. She wanted him to know that she was okay. And she offered to write a column about the entire, lurid episode. It was what any good journalist would do.

But her editor would hear nothing of it.

"I'll have a reporter call you. You can relate what happened in your own words, and the reporter will then write it up—in a hard-news story. Then you're taking time off."

"Okay," she said softly, with no argument. "Thank you, Richard."

The East Side of Lauderdale

By late afternoon, the commotion started to subside. While wandering around the aircraft ramp near the 737, trying to pull herself together, Kasey dialed up her squad commander in Fort Lauderdale. She knew he had been filled-in by the feds, so now it was time to get a read on her status. She was hoping against hope that she wouldn't be reprimanded yet again, suspended, or even discharged.

"Actually, the FBI guys gave you all the credit for finding those women, so you're to be highly commended for that," the commander said. "But we got other problems."

"I know," she said quietly. "I took the chopper without authorization and never called for backup."

"That's the least of it," he said.

"What do you mean?"

"You need to go with the federal marshals there. They'll transport you back for questioning. Then there's going to be a full IAD investigation."

"What? Why?"

"We have reason to believe you are involved in the death of Detective Peterson, who was found in a parking lot at the Palm-Aire condo complex. A witness saw him fall from a chopper. We think your chopper."

She turned and saw two marshals nonchalantly staring back, apparently waiting till she got off the phone before moving in.

"No need to investigate," she muttered. "I did it."

She clicked off the phone and walked over to the marshals.

25.

By nightfall, the palatial home of Clayton McGreggor was surrounded. Heavily armed police teams took positions behind vehicles and trees and on nearby rooftops. Dozens of other uniformed officers blocked off all streets leading into the ritzy neighborhood on the East Side of Fort Lauderdale.

Working off Kasey's information, investigators determined that McGreggor was indeed the kingpin of the operation that whisked well-to-do women to North Carolina to be videotaped being forcibly raped. Warrants were issued to arrest McGreggor and any accomplices.

Once everyone was in place, a police commander barked orders into a megaphone for McGreggor to give up and come out with his hands up. But there was no response. Attempts to reach him by phone also were unsuccessful.

A SWAT team burst into the sprawling twelve-bedroom house from three sides, wielding high-

The East Side of Lauderdale

powered automatic weapons and yelling, "Down! Police! Get down!"

They were expecting to be greeted by McGreggor's henchmen and gunfire. But much to their amazement, it was eerily quiet inside. They still exploded into room after room, but found no sign of McGreggor or his men, which contradicted intelligence that he was here somewhere.

Finally, they came upon a locked door on the second floor. Inside, they could hear the muffled groans and screams of a woman. They mounted their forces, fully expecting a standoff. They pounded down the door, and no less then ten men barged into the room, which turned out to be a nicely furnished and sizeable law study.

The police were prepared to spray bullets at anything that moved. Instead, their jaws dropped.

For there was McGreggor, wearing only a bathrobe spread wide open. He was calmly sitting in an easy chair, puffing on a cigar, a snifter of brandy on a side-table. Despite the furious commotion that suddenly burst upon him, he kept his eyes glued to a wide-screen television showing a video of Betty Sue Curtis being attacked. And he was vigorously fondling himself.

Adding to the bizarre scene, restaurateur Kenton Cook and high-powered attorney Bradley Crawford sat on either side of McGreggor. They, too, wore only bathrobes and had their hands busy at their crotches.

Broward State Attorney Harold Forest rushed in seconds after the SWAT team and was incredulous to see his breakfast buddies partaking in such lewd behavior. He already had been horrified to learn that

Ken Kaye

his so-called friends were behind the abductions of six women and likely the murder of Sidney Simon.

Seeing Forest's amazement, Kenton Cook, with a wide, mischievous grin, said, "Harold, if we thought you could still get it up, we would have asked you to join the party."

All were quickly arrested before reaching a conclusion.

26.

Three weeks after he underwent emergency surgery at the Asheville hospital, Bruce was transferred from intensive care to a private room. Although a swarm of news people and police investigators sought to talk to him, he permitted only one visitor.

When Kasey walked into his room on a sunny Tuesday late morning, a large purse slung over a shoulder, she beamed. She was amazed at how good he looked. His eyes were bright, his hair was combed and his face was clean-shaven. This was despite bullets puncturing a lung and a major artery in his upper leg, the amount of permanent damage still unknown.

She leaned down and pecked his cheek. He still had an IV in his right wrist and wires from his chest to a heart monitor, which displayed his rhythms. Outside, three levels down on the street, a bus gunned its engine and a car horn honked.

"You look wonderful," she remarked.

"Which is to say what, you'd never know I nearly got my butt blown away?"

She smiled politely.

"Yes, exactly."

"The wonders of modern medicine and doting nurses. You'll have to forgive me, I'm still in the dark on a few things. They did tell me one of the women didn't make it."

Kasey put her purse on his tray table and gingerly sat on the side of his bed. She had flown in from Fort Lauderdale that morning for this visit and planned to fly back that afternoon.

"That's right. But the rest did, and they've all been released from the hospital and reunited with their families. You saved a lot of lives, Jeff, including mine."

He looked down for a moment, and she thought she saw him blush.

"What about you, Kasey? Are you okay?"

She chuckled, somewhat morosely.

"I guess. They're still deciding whether to charge me for stealing the helicopter or reward me for helping to find the women."

"I'm sure it will be the latter."

"I'm not worried. I've got a lot of support from other officers, the union, and even the media. In the meantime, until my fate is decided, I'm off the job. With pay, luckily."

"That's not so bad." Then he looked around and lowered his voice. "Did they find Jed?"

She giggled at his attempt to be discreet.

"No need to be secretive, Jeff. I told them everything. How Jed jumped on the helicopter and tried to choke and shoot me. How I tried to put down

The East Side of Lauderdale

but that we had no choice but to swing the door into him, causing him to fall."

Bruce put up a hand.

"You mean how I swung the door into him. If there's culpability, it's on me."

"There's no culpability anywhere, Jeff. You saved both our lives because he was about to shoot us. I told the investigators that. After they saw the bullet hole in the chopper window, they bought it. It's been ruled self-defense."

Bruce exhaled.

"Glad to hear that. Tell me about the men they arrested. I heard something on TV that quite an influential ring was involved in making those videos."

She told him how Clayton McGreggor had hired Petrucco to arrange the abductions and produce videos of the rapes initially as a form of entertainment for himself and the old men in a breakfast club—Sheryl Tucker's breakfast club.

"The breakfast club members paid Petrucco a hundred thousand per video. It was pocket change for all of them," she said. "Dirty old men. They wanted to get Sheryl on tape all along. It was one of the reasons she was welcomed to their table. And she considered them dear friends."

"Wow."

She further explained that Petrucco convinced McGreggor that the tapes should be mass-produced and sold for big bucks on the black market.

"For that reason, the victims didn't have to endure just one rape but several, each attack becoming its own sequel video, for instance, Melissa Norman parts one, two, three and so on. By the time we got to them, each woman already had four or five videos made."

"Jesus. What was going to happen to the women, ultimately? That is, if they hadn't been found?"

Kasey frowned, unable to hide her disgust.

"Petrucco and McGreggor wouldn't say, but the investigators think in their final videos they would have been killed while being raped. Those tapes would have gone for a huge price."

Bruce shook his head.

"Did the police figure out why they always selected a victim after their photo appeared in the *East Lauderdale Tattler*?"

"McGreggor said it was his idea. He liked the way the *Tattler* presented stories on the women with big, complimentary photos. Better then the *Fort Lauderdale Post*, anyway."

"Why only businesswomen?"

"Simply put, it was a fetish," Kasey explained. "McGreggor told the detectives that rich, successful women were what turned him and the others on. Maybe it was an anger thing, their way of getting back at their bossy wives."

Bruce shook his head, thinking about that.

"Where did those guys Brad and Ray come from?"

"They were your garden-variety drug-running pilots. Petrucco signed them on because neither had a rap sheet. In addition to flying the 737, they were only too happy to plan the abductions and make hard-core videos."

"Petrucco was arrested?"

The East Side of Lauderdale

"Same night McGreggor was. Both he and McGreggor spilled their guts, hoping for leniency. But they're going away for life."

Bruce nodded.

"Sheryl. Is she okay?"

"She was shaken. But she returned to her job a few days ago and finally came out with a column about the whole thing."

Kasey grabbed her purse and pulled out a copy of the *Fort Lauderdale Post*. Tucker's column was stripped across the top under the headline:

THANKS TO REPORTER, ABDUCTED WOMEN, INCLUDING ME, RESCUED

It went into detail how Bruce's investigation led to the women and how, along with Kasey, he had prevented Tucker from being raped and killed. Typical of Tucker, it also included background on how Bruce had once been a respected reporter at a big newspaper and took a fall. But she went on to say she admired him for making a comeback at a small paper and finding redemption.

Bruce read it and looked up at Kasey.

"Figures. She beats me again ... on my own story," he mumbled.

Kasey smiled.

"Sheryl told me to tell you that the moment you feel up to it, you and I are invited to go to her house for a thank-you dinner. She insists."

He cocked his left eyebrow.

"That's going to be a while, Kasey. I'm in pretty bad shape."

She came over, leaned down and kissed him more earnestly.

"I hope not that long."

27.

On a breezy April evening, Bruce and Kasey walked up to the front door of an elegant two-story home in Las Olas Isles, an exclusive neighborhood of multi-million-dollar homes, yachts and deep canals east of downtown Fort Lauderdale. They were holding hands.

He wore a Navy blue blazer, khaki pants and Docksider shoes. He sported a neatly trimmed goatee, which he had grown during long days and weeks of physical rehabilitation. And he relied on a cane for balance, as he walked with a perceptible limp.

She, meanwhile, had on a sleeveless, black dress and pearls around her neck. In high heels, she, as usual towered over him. Her thick, black hair was pulled back into a bob in back, while long bangs fell over her forehead.

He rang the doorbell and Tucker opened the door.

"Jeff!" She hugged him, then Kasey. "Come in! Drinks are being served."

As promised, this was Tucker's celebratory dinner party in Bruce's honor. At his request she had kept it small affair.

Closing the front door, Tucker, wearing a dark-red evening gown, directed Bruce and Kasey to her den. There, an immaculately groomed Richard Bloom, wearing a lime-green jacket and bright-white pants, swirled vodka on the rocks and chatted with Bob Tucker, who wore a dark suit and sipped on bourbon.

"My, you both look lovely. Welcome," Bob Tucker said.

"Hello, hello," Bloom chimed in.

After two drinks worth of small talk, Tucker ordered everyone to the dinner table. She had hired two women caterers to prepare and serve the meal. Once everyone was seated, the caterers, wearing blue dresses with white smocks, came out of a swinging door connecting the dining room with the kitchen. They placed hefty shrimp cocktails before each person and offered either a red or white wine. That was followed with tomato broth and the main course: plates groaning with beef tenderloin, smothered in peppercorn sauce, with au-gratin potatoes and green beans.

"It was really good of you to do this, considering I am *still* your competition," Bruce said to Tucker, finishing his glass of white wine, which one of the caterers noticed and immediately refilled.

Some chuckles around the table.

"Well, you did save my life. I thought this was more appropriate than a thank-you note," Tucker said, arousing more smiles.

She then raised her wineglass.

The East Side of Lauderdale

"A toast to Jeff Bruce." Everyone hoisted glasses while she continued, "Jeff, I'll always be grateful to both you and Kasey for never giving up, for finding me and the others on that horrible day, and giving us all a second chance. I thank you from the bottom of my heart. I only hope that you and I can knock heads again on another big story—although, I hope not *quite* as big as this last one."

There was some light laughter.

"Here, here," Bob Tucker said.

"I'll drink to that," Richard Bloom said.

"Cheers," added Kasey.

Glasses clinked, they all took a sip, and the guests picked up their silverware to resume the feast.

Bruce nodded at Tucker.

"Thank you, Sheryl. I hope so, too. But that's going to be a while. My boss has made me her assistant editor for now, seeing as how I can't really do much street reporting with this bum leg."

"Hey, that's great," Bloom remarked, after carefully inserting a fork full of beef in his mouth. "That's a promotion, isn't it?"

"Yes, it is," Kasey answered for Bruce, displaying a prideful smile and taking his hand in plain view of the others.

"I'm just happy to be back at work, doing something," Bruce said. "By the way, Sheryl, thanks for that nice column you wrote about my first day back, the other day. I didn't see that coming."

"That was a fun day," Tucker said.

"You must tell us about it, dearest," Bob Tucker said, eyeing her while working busily with knife and fork.

Though he said nothing offensive, it was all in the tone. Tucker looked at her husband and felt nothing but disdain. She suddenly regretted postponing the divorce. In the aftermath of the episode in North Carolina, she had been too rattled to do much of anything except take long walks, trying to put things in perspective. Apparently sensing her internal duress, Bob had given her lots of space. So she had held off retaining an attorney, in effect giving him another chance.

But it was failing miserably. Now she was not only considering divorce, but also Carlos Pena's invitation to join him at the Sheraton, which he had re-extended in the past week. However, he now was working in the basement of the Police Department, demoted from homicide detective to car-theft crimes.

She pointed at Bruce with the sharp end of her knife.

"You tell us about that day," she said.

Bruce raised an eyebrow.

"The long and short of it is, I return to work thinking the staff might throw some kind of little welcome-back thing. Instead, I limp into the newsroom and find every news outlet in the free world there, television stations, radio stations and wire services, all lying in wait. I didn't realize I was so popular."

There were more chuckles because that was an obvious understatement. Since being credited with finding the abducted women and playing a major role in

The East Side of Lauderdale

saving them, even the national media had interviewed him.

"Anyway," Bruce said, looking at Tucker, "I wanted to tell you, I was honored that you showed up that day."

"I was honored to be there."

More smiles all around.

"So," Bob Tucker said brazenly, chewing on the tenderloin, eyes darting back and forth from Bruce to Kasey, "are you two living together now?"

Kasey blushed.

"No. We're not quite that far along yet."

"How far along are you, then?" Bob Tucker persisted.

Now even Bruce turned red, and Tucker became agitated.

"Bob, that was kind of rude."

"Just asking what everyone wants to know."

Tucker glared at him before turning to Kasey.

"Just ignore him."

Sensing the tension, Kasey shrugged.

"It's okay. We're just taking it as it goes."

Bruce smiled and nodded in agreement. As close as he and Kasey had become during the mission to North Carolina, his subsequent convalescence and rehabilitation had thrown cold water on their romance. Further, Kasey had been embroiled in a battle to keep her job. So, only a week earlier, after receiving his doctor's okay to return to the living again, he finally worked up the courage to ask her out on a for-real first date.

They had gone to a trendy club on Fort Lauderdale's beach, where everyone danced too fast and the music was too loud. Being a good sport, Bruce hobbled out onto the dance floor with his cane, swiveled his hips, and awkwardly flailed his arms, which made Kasey laugh. She liked how he made fun of himself.

Then there had been a slow dance, and she held him tight.

That night they had landed at his place—not hers—because she didn't want their first night of love to be in the same bed where she had endured the coarseness of Jed Peterson. With Bruce, she had savored a gentle touch, and they had been together every night since.

After Tucker's guests finished the main course, and as the caterers poured coffee, Bruce stood up, wobbled a bit, and caught himself. Kasey immediately stood up and grabbed him by the upper arm.

"You okay?"

Seeing the looks of concern around the table, Bruce held up a hand.

"I'm fine, folks. Every now and then I have trouble finding my balance. That's why I have to walk with this cane for awhile. Anyway, hope you'll excuse me. I need to use the little boy's room."

"Two doors down on the left side of the hall," Tucker said, adding coyly, "and be sure to leave a quarter."

"Ah, so you've raised your rates."

That drew more smiles, except from Kasey, who couldn't help feel something was wrong. As Bruce clopped away, he noticed Kasey was ready to follow him. He again held up a hand to say: I'm fine, really. She reluctantly retook her seat.

The East Side of Lauderdale

Down the hallway, Bruce found the bathroom, closed the door, and slid into a sitting position on the white-tile floor. He put his head in his hands, staving off a bout of intense upper-chest pain. The doctors told him it would eventually ease. But the deep ache continued to plague him, something to do with the still-healing tissues around the gunshot wound.

After a time, the pain faded and he pulled himself up, using his cane for leverage. He turned off the bathroom light and walked back into the hallway.

Then he saw it.

A painting on the wall directly opposite the bathroom showed a pleasant country scene, with background hills covered with green forests and misty streams. In the foreground was a lodge.

Bruce wrinkled his nose. The lodge looked remarkably similar to the one in North Carolina where the women had been held.

*

He studied a small, gold plaque on the bottom of the frame. In large capital letters, it read: "PINE MANOR." Below that was a short inscription: "Built in 1926 by the Carolina Central Railroad. Purchased in 2002 by Robert Tucker Enterprises, Inc."

Robert Tucker Enterprises, Bruce repeated in his mind. It was probably one of Bob Tucker's real estate holding companies. Then it dawned on him that it was the complete and formal title for RTE, Inc., the same company that owned the Boeing 737.

He looked more closely at the painting and noted how the front door windows were shaped, how the barrel-tile roof was styled. And he knew.

It was the same lodge.

His mind swirled with the implications of Bob Tucker owning the lodge where the women had been taken, raped and videotaped. His heart rate jumped when he thought of Kasey and Tucker now sitting at the same table with the man who might have engineered the entire setup.

He wasn't sure what to do next except try to act normal when he returned to the dinner table. But as he turned toward the dining room, he almost ran right into Bob Tucker, who had been standing there, observing him.

"See anything interesting?" Bob Tucker asked.

"No, not really, just admiring what a nice painting that is."

Bob Tucker smirked.

"Why don't we go back and join the party, then," he said evenly. He waited for Bruce to go down the hallway first.

*

As soon as Bruce sat down next to her, Kasey again sensed something wasn't right. His face was ashen and droplets of sweat were sprouting on his forehead. She reached to take his hand and found it clammy and cold.

"You okay?" she asked quietly.

Bruce nodded and picked up his spoon to sample the chocolate ice cream the caterers had set down. But

The East Side of Lauderdale

he put it right down, knowing he couldn't stomach a single bite. Kasey now knew something was very wrong.

But then Bob Tucker nonchalantly addressed her. He had his elbows on the table and his hands folded in front of him.

"Kasey, I understand things are going quite well for you now."

Kasey forced herself to look away from Bruce and focus on Bob Tucker.

"That's true, thanks to Sheryl and the columns she wrote about how the Police Department was on the verge of firing me because I violated some protocols. She made the bigwigs look small, considering my part in saving those women."

Sheryl Tucker smiled and said, "Not only did the City Commission end up giving Kasey an award for going above and beyond, but now she's flying regular daytime patrols."

"Again, many thanks, Sheryl," Kasey said.

She turned and looked at Bruce again.

Tucker did likewise and said, "You look a little peaked, Jeff. Feel okay?"

There was an uncomfortable silence before he answered.

"Actually, no. I don't."

"Was it something you ate?" Tucker asked.

"Actually, it was something he saw," Bob Tucker said.

Then he reached into his jacket and produced a .44 Magnum.

28.

Suddenly, the dinner table went quiet, and faces turned white.

Sheryl Tucker was incredulous.

"Bob? What's going on? What are you doing with that gun?"

Bob Tucker laughed, making an eerie sound, like a lonely goose honking in winter.

"Why don't you tell them," he said, nodding at Bruce.

Everyone turned to Bruce, who kept his eyes on Bob Tucker.

"Seems I've stumbled onto a dirty little secret."

"That being what?" Tucker asked, her anxiety obvious.

"That, all along, it was your husband who set up the abductions."

"What?" Tucker and Kasey yelped at the same time.

Bob Tucker honked again.

"Go on," he said to Bruce. "This is interesting."

The East Side of Lauderdale

Bruce swallowed. Sweat continued to stream from his forehead.

"My guess is that Clayton McGreggor never was the ringleader, just a front man. You probably paid him a hefty sum to develop that video operation, hire Frank Petrucco and the rest of it. McGreggor knew from the start that if he gave you up, you'd kill his family, or something to that effect."

Bob Tucker smirked.

"He happens to have two lovely daughters and seven grandchildren."

Bruce nodded and continued.

"So McGreggor took the fall and your name was never mentioned to the cops. I suspect Petrucco was in the same boat."

"He happens to have a lovely young wife," Bob Tucker said, then laughed again, with the horrible honking.

Bruce took a deeper look at the man.

"The question is, why did you feel the need to hurt so many people?"

Bob Tucker shrugged smugly.

Sheryl Tucker jumped up.

"You set this all up? Set me up to be abducted? Tied to a bed with a fishing bob in my mouth? Nearly raped? You son of a bitch!"

She began circling the table, intending to claw his eyes out. But Kasey and Bloom jumped up to stop her. Bob Tucker stopped smiling. He aimed the large-caliber gun at his wife's forehead. She stopped trying to get at him when she saw the black eye of the barrel staring at her.

"Bitch," he growled. "Sit down. Everyone, sit down!"

Tucker slowly retreated to her seat, restraining herself. Kasey and Bloom also settled back down.

"Why, Bob?" his wife asked, still heated. "Why did you do that to me? Why make those disgusting videos?"

Bob Tucker stared at her intolerantly.

"Perhaps you have yourself most to blame, Sheryl, dearest."

"Me? Why?"

Bob Tucker shrugged.

"Let's start with this. I'm just a man with all the normal impulses. So, when you refused to have anything to do with me, oh, about two years ago, I was forced to fantasize. Know what I mean?"

She breathed indignantly but remained silent.

"Which is to say, about the time you kicked me out of my own bedroom, I had to resort to pornography. Hell, if you weren't going to play with me, I had to play with myself."

He laughed at his own vulgarity, but seeing the stone-cold faces, he shrugged and continued.

"Anyway, the thing was, I found all those garden-variety videos rather trashy. The women in them are pathetic. So I sought something more satisfying for the soul. I soon discovered that if you put a high-class, respectable woman in the same position, it's much more gratifying."

Tucker crossed her brow.

"How did you discover that?"

Bob Tucker shrugged again.

The East Side of Lauderdale

"Interesting story. About the time things went south for us, dearest, this young CEO of an investment firm sashays into my boardroom. Let me tell you, she was a magnificent creature, all dressed up in a business outfit, diamonds and gold all over the place, long blond hair and a million-dollar smile."

Bob Tucker broadened his own smile, recalling that day.

"The thing was, she knew was hot. As if we needed verification, the *East Lauderdale Tattler* had just done a big spread on her, which her associates made sure we knew by passing out copies of the damn thing. So, she's feeling pretty good about herself and comes on like gangbusters, saying she intends to buyout one of our telecommunications firms, and we would be fools not to play along.

"Much to her surprise, we turn her down, and she throws a real power-bitch fit. She threatens an anti-trust suit, implies my financial advisors are idiots and calls me an old fool. If it was her intention to piss me off, she succeeded. And it wasn't so much because of the attitude, but rather because I plainly resented the hell out of her.

"See, I'm an old-fashioned guy, worked damn hard to get where I am and believe that everyone else should have to work hard to earn their lot in life. But this persnickety, little bitch obviously had been given all her power, position and status based on the fact she looked good in an Ann Taylor get-up.

"Anyway, because I'm a gentleman, during the meeting, I was civil. Never let her know how annoyed I was at her tactics. But after the meeting, I had a drink with Clayton McGreggor, who has always been a good business associate, and told him about how the bitch insulted me. I remarked that she wouldn't be so uppity if you ripped her out of that tight skirt and put her in her place.

"Of course, I was only joking. But Clayton said if I wanted to spend the money, he could make it happen. I figured, what the hell?"

"Oh my God," Sheryl Tucker muttered.

"So, as Jeff postulated, McGreggor set it up at my behest," Bob Tucker continued. "He hired Petrucco, who was reputed to be the biggest producer of so-called legit rape videos in the porn industry. And Petrucco hired Brad and Ray, a pair of drug runners by trade, to be both our pilots and video actors. They were perfect because they knew how to avoid getting caught.

"And, for a price, they did something extra: They would stake out the power bitches to see what they wore to work and procure some of their wardrobe, right down to the exact size. In that way, on video, they would be reduced from important corporate officers to subservient little wenches.

"So, as you might guess, the snippy blonde was our first target. Wish I could remember her name, something like Susanna. You should have heard her squeal on tape. It made for fabulous entertainment. In fact, McGreggor and I enjoyed it so much that we decided to go after more power bitches.

"And it also was at that point that McGreggor suggested we expand our little circle as a means to defray our costs. He said he felt comfortable sharing the videos with other members of his breakfast club.

The East Side of Lauderdale

All except Harold Forest, that is, because, well, he's a prosecutor. We eventually came to realize that putting these videos on the black market would be hugely profitable. But that scheme, of course, went out the window with the raid in North Carolina. Ah well, another time, perhaps. Questions, anyone?"

The group was wide-eyed, mouths agape.

"My God," Sheryl Tucker whispered.

"Incredible," Kasey mumbled.

Bloom, shaking his head, asked, "What happened to that first woman?"

"We killed her," Bob Tucker said matter-of-factly. "At the time the media made a deal out of it, suspecting her boyfriend murdered her. But without a body, to this day, she's only considered a missing person."

He let out more horrible honking, then settled back to smile at the terrified reaction of his dinner guests. All quickly figured out that they now were in serious danger; Bob Tucker likely wouldn't allow a murder confession to leave his home.

His wife put her face in her hands. Bloom, sitting next to her, put an arm around her shoulder and dropped his head.

"Why do this in North Carolina? Why not here?" Kasey asked quietly.

Bob Tucker raised an eyebrow.

"Good question. To do authentic rape videos, Petrucco needed a very remote location, a place where the victims would never be found, where the police would never come sniffing. The lodge was perfect. You have to drive over miles of winding mountain roads to even get to the entrance road. The same road you landed on, incidentally, Kasey."

"So you also built the runway there just for this sick operation?" she asked.

"Actually, the runway was already there when I bought it. I just expanded it to accommodate my personal Boeing 737, the perfect vehicle to transport the women."

Bruce asked, "How was it that RTE, your own personal ghost corporation, owned the 737, but the authorities didn't trace the plane back to you? Or the lodge, for that matter, since it was also titled to RTE."

Bob Tucker now swung the gun nonchalantly at Bruce.

"Easy. My name isn't anywhere in the corporate papers. The official CEO, if you would have checked, was listed as Juan Castillo."

"Who's he?"

"The janitor in my downtown office building."

Bruce grimaced, angry with himself for not following through on that angle.

"Did the men in Sheryl's breakfast club actually select the women, as McGreggor told the police, or was it you?"

"Me, all along," Bob Tucker confessed. "I selected only women who appeared in the *Tattler*, I guess in honor of that first power bitch. But, indeed, the paper does present these women as larger than life, so successful and so pretty. But the way I see it, the more successful and pretty a woman is, the more satisfying it is to see her humiliated."

"Oh, my God," Tucker whispered again.

Bob Tucker nonchalantly aimed the gun back at his wife's head.

"What's funny, Sheryl, dearest, is that the moment you joined their group, your old breakfast friends wanted to see you ripped out of your clothing, captured on tape. But I told them no, that would be too risky, draw too much attention to the operation. So, in essence, I saved you, at least until you went snooping into my affairs. Then, you presented us with a golden opportunity to make you a featured performer. And I was so looking forward to that—until this fool right here spoiled everything."

He swung the gun in Bruce's direction.

Bruce remained quiet, aching, sweating and sensing that this was where the going got rough.

"Bottom line is I've been deprived of that ultimate video," Bob Tucker said, his voice growing intense. "But I figure we can rectify that if you two, Jeff and Sheryl, do the nasty, right here."

He patted the top of the dinner table.

"You've got to be kidding," Tucker cried, unable to hide her outrage. "You're crazy! Can't you see that, Bob? You are out-of-your-head crazy!"

Bob Tucker enjoyed seeing his wife squirm.

"Sheryl, dearest, you might think that's kind of a crude request. But surely by now you've figured out that I'm the type who likes to watch. I'm sure the rest of these fine people would like to observe, too."

The door to the kitchen swung open and the two caterers came out to pick up plates. Bob Tucker swiveled his gun and pulled the trigger twice, the blasts loud and alarming. Both women were hit in the chest, emitting grunts of surprise. Then they fell dead, blood oozing onto their white smocks.

*

Tucker screamed. Bloom and Bruce instinctively pushed back from the table. Kasey froze but desperately wished she had brought a gun. Meanwhile, the smell of acrid gun smoke filled the air.

Bob Tucker honked, seeing all their reactions.

Tears flowing again, Tucker clenched her hands at her chest.

"Jesus, Bob, what the hell are you doing?"

Bob Tucker's nostrils fared.

"Shut up, you castrating bitch. You don't think you deserve this? You've done nothing but make me feel small and impotent the entire time we've been married. Like I had some sort of disease."

"Bob, I'm sorry if—"

"Know what really pisses me off? You put me off so you could do this fag here." He pointed the gun at Bloom. "That's why you had to work late all those nights, wasn't it Sheryl? So you could screw your editor?"

She shook her head.

"That's not true, Bob. I never did anything of the sort. I was never unfaithful. How could you think such a thing?"

"Because he's a small man," Bloom said with obvious contempt. "And small men demand attention."

Bob Tucker carefully aimed the gun at Bloom's face.

"Foolish words from a fag," he sneered.

The East Side of Lauderdale

Kasey cautiously held up a hand.

"Bob. Please. Calm down. Let's not do anything—"

"Shut up!" Bob Tucker yelled at her. "This isn't a negotiation. Now, for the last time, Sheryl and Jeff, get the hell out of those clothes or die, here and now!"

Tears streaming down her cheeks, Tucker reached back to unzip her dress. Bruce stood up slowly, relying on his cane, and took off his jacket.

Kasey also stood up, carefully.

"Sit down!" Bob Tucker barked at her, shifting the gun in her direction.

"Okay, in a minute. But I want to ask you something, Bob. Why would you leave such blatant evidence like a painting of that lodge in this house? You were taking quite a risk, weren't you?"

Bruce realized what Kasey was doing—buying time. But he wasn't sure what she had in mind.

"You know, you're really quite pretty," Bob Tucker said, ignoring her question. "Tall, black women do something for me. Before this night is over, let's you and I get to know each other better. A lot better."

He burst out laughing and honking, seeing Kasey's glare. But that's when Bruce saw the gleam of light reflecting off an object in Kasey's hand.

Bruce rapped his cane loudly on top of the dinner table.

"Hey, you son of a bitch, no way am I going to let you touch my woman."

He took an aggressive step forward and swung the cane back like it was a baseball bat.

Bob Tucker ceased his laughter and turned the gun in Bruce's direction.

Which gave Kasey the opportunity she was looking for. With all her strength, she heaved a seven-inch steak knife into Bob Tucker's chest. For whatever reason, the now-murdered caterers had failed to pick it up from the table after the main course.

It thudded in with the sound of a cleaver slicing into a ripe cantaloupe.

Bob Tucker groaned and looked at the handle, protruding from his heart. He started falling backwards, but still had the wherewithal to point his gun at his wife.

Bloom, who was closest to Sheryl Tucker, saw this and lunged, putting himself between Bob and Sheryl Tucker.

Then there was another ringing gunshot.

Bloom seized up as the bullet ripped into his right, upper chest.

He grasped at the wound, blood coating his hands, gushing onto his lime-green jacket, then he collapsed on the floor, almost on top of Bob Tucker.

"Jesus!" cried Sheryl Tucker, and she immediately ran to Bloom's side.

"Jeff, call nine-one-one!" Kasey yelled, then charged over to Bob Tucker to pull the gun from his hand. But it was clear that he was no longer a threat. His eyes had gone blank and blood trickled out of the corner of his mouth.

Using his cane, Bruce clopped into the kitchen, found a phone and made the call for help.

Bloom looked up into Tucker's eyes as she cradled his head.

"Don't die, Richard, please," she whispered.

The East Side of Lauderdale

"I wouldn't think of it," he rasped. "I love you too much."

She looked at him with a sad smile.

"I should have seen that … "

Ten minutes later, the police and paramedics arrived. They were able to stabilize Bloom, but he was in critical condition. Tucker accompanied him as he was taken by ambulance to the hospital, holding his hand the whole way. But before she left her house, she took a moment to spit on her deceased husband.

*

Several hours later, well after midnight, the detectives finally sorted everything out and secured the scene. Three bodies were carted out in black bags, and it was quickly determined that Kasey had acted justifiably in killing Bob Tucker.

But she was glassy-eyed from the trauma.

Seeing her distress, Bruce gently led her out of the Tuckers' home and walked her to his car.

"You know, you look like you could use a vacation," he said as he opened the passenger-side door for her.

Rather than get in, she looked at him blankly, saying nothing.

"I was thinking maybe we'd go hiking in the mountains of Carolina."

She kept looking at him for several seconds before she blinked. When he cocked his head, waiting for an answer, she cracked a faint smile.

"Very funny," she muttered.

"Then how about a cruise to St. Thomas?"

She suddenly put her arms around him and hugged hard. He thought she might cry, but she kept holding him, rocking gently side to side.

"How about we just go home," she said softly, her face buried in his shoulder.

"Where's home?"

"Your apartment. I'm looking forward to sprucing the place up."

About the Author

Ken Kaye is a journalist based in South Florida.

Printed in the United States
35520LVS00001B/37-54